OBSESSION

Book One

S.M PHILLIPS

To My
Dickie!
Love you lots
DPhillips
xx

COPYRIGHT

authorised, associated with, or sponsored by the trademark owners.

BOOKS BY S.M PHILLIPS

~ Escape down under (Down Under #1)
~ Fallen down under (Down Under #2)

~ Obsession (Obsession #1)

To my Betsy Boo,

You're amazing, and I love you very much.
Thanks for everything.

ANNA

"Sorry? I'm really struggling to hear you." The music is so loud that I'm struggling to do the one thing that I get paid to do. "I still can't hear you, could you try shouting a little louder?" I ask as I try to lip read from the guy stood just inches away from me, but it's no good.

"Two. Double. Vodka's." He shouts, pausing between each word.

"Coming right up." I say, finally understanding what he's after. I glance at the clock and see that it's almost time for last orders to be called and I can't wait to get out of this hell hole. It's been one long arse day and I can't wait to put it all behind me and climb into bed. The sooner I can save up enough money to head out of here the better. I came to stay here with my cousin, Holly, until I found myself again; but what did she do? She only went and disappeared three months later; leaving me to take care of the mess that she'd left behind. So, every day without fail, I come to Temptation like the mug that I am, in the hope that today will finally be the day for some decent tips and, on the off chance that Holly might just come waltzing back through that door. Bloody wishful thinking, but still, a girl can dream right?

"And grab one for yourself beautiful."

"Thanks." I smile at him knowing full well that I won't be taking him up on his offer. I'm not the type of girl to drink on the job, especially in this place. Sure the locals may well be harmless but there's only me and Joey here most nights now that Holly's done a runner and he's constantly off his tits. I'm amazed that he even shows up most of the time. I really don't know when I'll hear from Holly. The last I heard from her was a few weeks back, but as long as she pays my wage, and keeps up with her bills, then I'm kind of happy. I slip my tip into the jar by the till and hand Mr Eager his change.

"So lady, you work here often? I'm sure I'd remember a pretty face like yours."

"Every goddamn night, sunshine. Maybe you wanna take that drink to your girlfriend over there before she sits on that guys cock." I chuckle to myself as his head whips around so fast, I'm surprised he doesn't do himself an injury. Working in a bar, you see everything and most of it is that hideous, you start to question

what you look like when you've had one too
many yourself.

"Joey. Get your goddamn arse over here!"
I shout as my eyes find his over the other side of
the bar.
"Keep your pants on woman, what's
wrong with you? You never heard of havin' a
little bit of fun?" He shouts back at me.
"You ever heard of earning your keep?
Move it." I snap. The bar's filling up pretty quickly
and all he cares about, is grinding against the
nearest woman or two. Shit really needs to
change around here and fast. It takes him a
couple of more minutes to fully pry himself away
from his latest victim, while I still try to attend to
our punters. I feel his arms snake around my
hips and I automatically flinch at the contact.
"Back off, Joe. I'm not in the mood for your
bullshit tonight. You do nothing but fuck around
and piss our profits up the wall. All while I'm left
to do the fucking work. Shit man, when did you
last clean this place? It's disgusting."
"Ah, lighten up will you." He smiles back
at me. The guy really has no clue. None,
whatsoever.
"Whatever, Joe. Just pull your finger out is
all I ask, 'Kay?" I hate getting mad at him, but I
guess someone has to. It's just been me and him
for as long as I can remember running this place,
and it isn't half wearing thin on me. I try to keep
him in check as best I can, but he's male,
surrounded by booze and women left, right and

centre. I throw my hands up in despair, finally admitting to myself that's there's just no controlling him. Whatsoever.

"Just chill Anna. Loosen up a bit. Who knows, you might even enjoy it." He winks at me, and I want to slap him in the face so bad. Why does he have to be such a jerk? All I want him to do is take some goddamn responsibility for a change.

"Yeah, maybe. Tonight's not going to be the night that I find out though." I point at the heaving bar. Fridays are normally quite busy but tonight is utter madness. Looking out past the bar, all I can see before me is a mass of grinding bodies. It may well be some time before they all leave.

Finally, once the majority of the crowd has dispersed, I begin to carry out the joyous task of cleaning up after everyone. I shouldn't be surprised when I spot Joey throwing back some shots over at the bar.

"For fuck sake, Joe. Can you not give it a rest for five bloody minutes?"

"Here, have one. Stop being so uptight and relax. Having fun is good for you. It releases endorphins and shit." I step closer to him as a mischievous grin spreads across his face. Oh what the hell... One won't hurt and if it shuts him up for a little bit, then I'm game. I guess a little distraction never hurt anyone.

"Okay. Pour 'em." Pulling myself up on a bar stool Joey hands me my shot and I quickly throw it back before I can change my mind. The burn instantly hits the back of my throat and it feels like it's on fire. I can't help but choke out a cough from the assault that it's causing.

"Damn girl. Here, another one will take care of that." He says, like it's medicine.

"I'm not too sure. I think one's way more than enough for me. Jeez, how do you drink this shit all the time anyways?" I don't know how he can talk after he's drank this shit, it's absolutely vile.

"It's like anything... You get used to it over time."

"Well, in that case, pour me another, and keep them coming." This shit is horrible, but if it allows me to escape from my wandering mind for just a little while, then I'll take the hit.

I don't know how long we've been seated here at the bar, doing shots and putting the world to rights, but my vision is slightly blurred and for once I don't feel the huge weight of pressure that is usually present on my shoulders. I feel relaxed and dare I say it, slightly happy. Even the sight of Joey isn't pissing me off, which makes a welcome change. It's been a long time since I drank and I'm a little scared to move from my position on the bar stool, worried that I'll end up falling flat on my arse. The last thing I want to do is go arse over tit and give Joey an excuse to take the piss out of me for weeks, if not months to come.

"What's your story Anna?" I try to focus

my gaze on Joe but the straining of my eyes hurts my head way too much and makes me more dizzy.

"Story?" I ask with a slight frown. "I don't have a story to tell."

"Bullshit." I jump a little from the tone of his voice and my eyes stay firmly on his, as he watches me suspiciously. Bullshit it maybe, but my crazy shit stays with me and me alone. There is no reason for me to drag anyone else into the mess that I've found myself in. It's bad enough that I'm the one that's running from it. "You think I don't see the sadness in those pretty eyes?"

"Jesus Joe. Can't you just quit it? There's nothing to tell, just drop it." He holds his hands up above his head in surrender at the venom in my voice, and I think he knows not to push me any further on the matter. One of these days, people might just learn how to mind their own goddamn business. "How the hell are we supposed to get home now?" I ask, eager to change the subject.

"We could always crash here, or how about my truck? We could get really cosy in there, sweet thing."

"Over my dead body Joe. I've got a better idea. How about you call a cab while I shift the evidence?" Why, oh, why did I agree to do shots in the first place? With Joey of all people. As soon I get my hands on Holly I'm going to fucking kill her for leaving me with all this shit to deal with on my own.

"Don't be such a killjoy, Anna. You should

let loose sometimes and enjoy yourself." He smirks at me while filling yet more shot glasses. His stomach must be made of steel or some shit. He raises his glass and asks, "Another?"

"Not for me. I told you already, I'm heading home. I'm back here tomorrow for another joyful shift." I say sarcastically. Hopefully, with a clear head. There's nothing worse than working on a hangover, and it's been a while since that happened to me. "You coming or not?"

The cold hits me as soon as we step outside. One of these days I'll remember to bring a coat with me when I leave the house. I turn and see Joey heading in the opposite direction, stumbling on his shaky legs as the alcohol takes over his body, while the cold night air hits him. I guess he'd be pretty hot if he wasn't such a slut. He turns slowly, on unsteady legs and smiles at me as I finish locking the door.

"You sure you don't want to stay in my truck? This is your last chance to join me and see what those chicks dig so much. I can guarantee that you'll be begging me for some more of the good stuff."

As if right on cue, my taxi pulls up in front of me. "Keep wishing. I'm not feeling chlamydia right now. I'll let you know if I change my mind." I shout back at him, as I hop into the waiting vehicle, eager to get home and put another shit day to rest. I try Holly a couple of times while we drive, but it's pointless as I'm greeted with her goddamn voicemail once again.

Once I've finally made it home, I stagger the short distance up to my door and fiddle with the key in the lock for what feels like an age, until finally, I strike gold and the door opens for me, enticing me in to its warm, welcoming luxury. I don't waste any time when I step over the threshold. Today's been far too exhausting for anything but sleep, and that's what I plan to do.

After a couple of failed attempts trying to climb the stairs, I finally enter my room, toss my bag to the side, kick off my shoes and I climb into bed, waiting for the darkness to sweep over me. It's no good. I pull myself up and anxiously grab my phone from the side table to check for any missed calls or messages. I let out a long sigh of relief when the screen flashes up blank. I've changed my number numerous times, but it's never enough. The fear is still there; eating away at me, tearing me up inside, desperate for me to become nothing but a shell of emptiness.

Now that I've had alcohol in my system my mind is on overdrive and every sound has me on edge. Fucking Holly. I still can't believe she's actually left me here alone when she knew how much I needed her. That was the reason why I came here in the first place. *"You'll be safe here."* She said. Absolute fucking bollocks, that's what I call it.

I wake to the rain hammering down against the window, while the strong winds threaten to rip the house apart. How I miss the sun and warmth of California. Once I get this course out of the way, maybe I'll be able to go back home. One day maybe, but I'll be worse there than I am here and deep down I know it. *"Soak it up and weep girl."* I think to myself. *You ain't ever gonna get to go home, and you've only got yourself to blame for this hell of a mess that you're in.* Every day, I wish I could go back and listen to the people around me. Maybe if I had listened, I wouldn't have needed to run away in the first place and leave everyone and everything that I had ever known behind.

More final demands meet me at the door as I step towards the kitchen. I don't bother to open them anymore. I think I stopped after the first week once I'd become familiar with the envelopes and stamps. Plus, Holly's fully aware of them and if she doesn't want to deal with them, why should I? She's obviously too busy having fun to be worrying about her financial mess and I'm not prepared to keep dealing with her shit. I still feel a little twitchy and on edge from last night, but surprisingly there's not a hangover in sight. The constant fear still simmers away in the pit of my stomach and no matter what I do, it just won't go away. I just hope that one of these days, it gets easier. I really don't want to face the fact that I might need to see someone. No one needs to hear about my stupid lifestyle choices and dramas. I hit the shower before I decide to do anything. As the hot water sprays down against my skin, I will it to wash all my problems away.

Once I've made some fresh coffee, I decide that today is solely going to be spent catching up with my assignment. I've got extensions coming out of my arse and if I have any hope of passing this course, then I can't fall any further behind. I took the course as soon as I arrived here. It gave me something to look forward to, something to take my mind away from the constant worry and fear. I guess I saw it as a goal, a way to improve my life and to try and make something of myself, but so far all I have achieved is to royally fuck up some more. How did it get to this? I used to be so head-strong and always completed the stuff that I set my mind to, and now, it doesn't look like anything will ever go right.

I settle down at the kitchen table with my papers when a knock sounds at the door. Panic instantly consumes me. Fuck, fuck, fuck. What am I supposed to do? I take a few deep calming breaths and repeat *"calm down Anna, you're safe here."* Yet, the knocks on the door continue and I cautiously pull myself away from the table and slowly tread towards the door. Looking through the peephole of the old tattered wooden door, I try to make out the person stood on the opposite side; but it's almost impossible from the condensation that has collected over time. I've been telling Holly to get a new door for ages, but again she didn't listen to a word I said. Gathering every bit of strength that I have, I pull the door open and I'm instantly greeted by two men. I take in their smart suits as they stand before me. They look very serious and professional. Why are they here, and what the hell do they want with Holly, or me?

"Miss Jameson?" The shorter of the two asks. Oh fuck, no, this can't be happening. I knew that this would happen sooner or later and now they've actually got me cornered when I have no backup in sight.

"I'm afraid she's not here." I say shakily as the words automatically fall from my lips like they have so many times before. Lying has fast become my automatic response to most things these days.

"Not to worry Miss. If you could have her call us, it would be most appreciated." I nod and think they seem quite polite and friendly, but don't they all? Maybe they're not here to hunt me down and find me, but that doesn't mean I'm going to give my identity away anytime soon. No, that's something that I'll be keeping under wraps for as long as I can.

"I'll be sure to pass your message on." I say, as I plaster on a fake smile and go to close the door on the two men stood before me. All I want to do is run. Run and never look back and hide away from all this craziness that is now suddenly my life. The shorter man's hand shoots through the gap just before I close the door and I jump, suddenly scared for my safety.

"If you can get her to call that number we

should be able to move things along quite quickly. I'm sure she'll be glad once all this is over and done with Miss. We like things to go as smoothly as possible, I'm sure you understand?"

I have no idea who these two men are, but anxiety floods through me in waves. "Sure thing." I say politely while desperately wanting to shut the door and hide away from the rest of the world.

"Good day Miss." He nods and they both turn to retreat down the driveway. Once the door is firmly shut behind me and double bolted, I flip the business card over in my hand, but it means absolutely nothing to me. It looks expensive and very smart, just like those suits that they were wearing.

'Randall Letting Agency.' Is printed on the front in bold purple letters on a silky black background. What the hell would a letting agency want with me? How do they even know who I am? I'm undecided if I should call them or if it's someone actually trying to catch me out. Anything to do with this property should be going through Holly not me. Everything about this screams dodgy and I don't like it one little bit. Screw that, there's not a cat in hells chance that I'll be phoning them. Ever. I quickly toss the card in the bin. If they really want me, and it is to do with this house, then I'm sure they'll be back.

I make my way back into the kitchen once I've heard the car drive off. I pick up the phone from the side and desperately hope on the off chance that Holly picks up. It rings. I can't believe that it actually fucking rings, but surprise surprise, she doesn't answer. Fucking hell. I guess it's a start, normally when I ring it goes straight to voicemail. If it's ringing she must be checking it from time to time, maybe to check her messages or something, so I decide to do just that.

"Hey, Hol. It's me, but you already knew that right? I'm sure by now that you must have stumbled upon my numerous missed calls and messages. Maybe you could give me a call back real soon, you know, when you find the time in your new *wonderful, carefree, I'll just fuck everything off, because I can life*. I can only imagine that you're having heaps of fun with Hernandez or whatever he's called, but you've got some pretty big priorities that you need to take care of back here. Or has that shit completely skipped your mind? I'm beyond fucking pissed Holly, so do yourself a favour and call me back ASAP."

How can one person anger me so pissing much. Holly was always the one to have her head screwed on, and now? God, I don't know what's happened to her but she just doesn't give a toss about anyone or anything around her. I'm still baffled as to why she just upped and left with someone that she'd only met once or twice at Temptation. Suddenly it was love at first sight and she decided to head off on a *once in a lifetime* road trip with him to only god knows where and for who knows how long.

"He's come into my life for a reason Anna. I can feel it." She said a day before her drastic departure. "I need to go with my gut instinct on this. It's what I need right now and I don't want to look back on a bunch of *what if's* later on in my life, you know?" That was the last time I saw her. She soon packed her bags' hopped into his truck and disappeared into the sunset without a goddamn care in the world. Maybe we're not so different after all.

ANNA

Temptation is already lit up as I walk towards the door and I stop in surprise. Maybe Joey pissed the bed; either that or he's off his tits again. Never in the memory of man has Joey arrived here before me, let alone open up. He usually likes to wait until the *"fresh pussy"* has arrived. As I enter, the only sound comes from the jukebox in the corner and it's lights reflects against the wall mirrors surrounding the empty bar. I'm instantly on high alert when I don't see Joey anywhere and fear, mixed with adrenaline begin to consume me. This feeling is starting to happen much too frequently for my liking. It was supposed to get easier when I left to come here, not cripple my every move.

"Joey." I shout, while grabbing the nearest pool cue from the wall. It never hurt anyone to be prepared for an attack, especially it if was to prevent them from getting hurt first off. "Joey." I shout again, a little louder this time, suddenly feeling more confident now that I'm armed. Shit, I hope he's here and playing some kind of sick joke on me. Maybe he's changing the barrels or something. "Shit Joey where are you?" I mutter as I step closer to the bar. Out of the corner of my eye, I see a dim light coming from the office door which is slightly open ajar. Why would Joey be in the office? He doesn't even have a key. At least, not to my knowledge anyway. My whole gut reaction is telling me to take a step back, but curiosity gets the better of me. Wasn't it curiosity that always killed the cat?

"You're late." A deep rustic voices booms around the room. I look slowly to my right and see him stood there watching me, one eyebrow raised as if daring me to argue with him.

"And you are...?" I ask, a little taken aback at this ruggedly beautiful intruder. I watch him more closely noticing how his deep brown eyes dance in the light. Eyes that promise both danger and excitement.

"I didn't ask you a question, so quit talking and get out there and do your job."

I should be scared with the tone that he is using towards me and I should be backing off like he says. Instead, I'm rooted to the spot and I find myselfl wanting to know who the hell this guy is, and what he thinks he's doing shouting his orders about in my office.

"Excuse me?" My hands fall to my hips as I wait for him to look at me again, maybe take in the pool cue that's still in my hand, but he doesn't even bother to look up. Instead he continues to rummage for something in the pile of boxes that are positioned next to him. My eyes are drawn instantly to his biceps, working overtime with each move that he makes. Jeez, he's well-built and I struggle to pull my eyes away from that body.

"I don't like being spoken to in that tone. You hear me lady? If you know what's fucking good for you, then you'll turn that sweet arse of yours back around and get behind that goddamn bar and work." He snarls at me.

What an absolute arsehole. Who the fuck does this guy think he is? I automatically pull my phone out from my bag, unsure what I'm actually going to do with it. Do I call the police? Report him for trespassing?

"Who are you gonna call, Holly?" He laughs and the smile that dances across his face has me feeling a mixture of emotions, and I don't like a single one of them.

"You know Holly?" I whisper. Disbelief floods through me. How can he know Holly? Shitting hell, he bloody does as well. He must have spoken to her recently too. As I stand with my mouth hanging open, I realise he isn't going to answer me anytime soon, if ever; so instead, I set my shoulders firmly, and say, "When you speak to her again, tell her from me to get her goddamn arse back home and sort her fucking shit out pronto." before turning on my heels and storming out of the office.

Temptation begins to fill up quite fast and I'm not complaining about it. At least this way my mind has a welcome distraction from the uber, obnoxious, yet sexy as hell creature that has invaded my place of work. I look up from wiping the bar down and see Joey snaking his way through the crowd, smiling and pleasing the women as he passes. As soon as he sees me, I beckon him over with a slight wave.

"So who's the dick in the office?" I ask as he approaches me.

"Who Jensen? Ah shit, I knew I meant to tell you something last night."

"No shit. How did something like that skip your mind? What's he even doing here? How the hell does he even have a key to the office? And why is he such an arrogant arse?"

Joey runs his hand down his face before answering me and I instantly know that I'm not going to like what he's about to tell me. "So you've still not spoken to Holly, huh?"

"What's Holly got to do with any of this Joe?" My mind is completely frazzled from all of this crazy shit that seems to be happening. None of this is making any bloody sense to me... At all. "Quit keeping me in the dark and just tell me what you need to tell me." I snap.

"I really thought she would have told you

by now Anna..." He cuts off while he reaches behind us for some shot glasses. "I don't know how to break this to you, but; she's sold Temptation."

"What?" I stare at him like he's just grown two heads. I can't believe the words that I am hearing. There is no way that Holly would ever sell this place. This is her baby. Nothing and no one could ever come between this place and her. I begin to laugh at Joe, waiting for the punch line, but nothing comes. Instead, he just continues to look at me with pitty in his eyes. "You're having me on aren't you? If so, now really isn't a good time for your games so quit messing around."

"I'm telling you the truth Anna. I wish I wasn't, but damn straight, she sold it last week." He says, while looking me straight in the eye before knocking back his shot.

"Wait a minute. You knew about this? You fucking knew all this time and didn't tell me? Jesus Christ Joey. What the hell goes on in that goddamn head of yours? Jeez." I shout and shake my head at him.

"I pay you to work, not to stand around gossiping like old fucking women and taking the royal piss. All I can hear is you two yipping at each other from in there and it's fucking irritating as hell. Joey, fix me a double while you're stood there doing jack shit."

Who the hell does this guy think he is? There is no way that I'm going to stand here and listen to this bullshit that's pouring from this pricks mouth. I haven't worked my backside off to get this bar back off the ground, just to be ordered around by an obnoxious, arrogant bastard. What right does he have coming in here and calling the shots? Apparently this is the guy that Holly's sold it to my arse. There's no way in hell that she'd hand this place over to a jerk like him.

"Yeah, do as your told, Joe." I say sarcastically to him. "I'm outta here." I'm beyond furious right now and he doesn't even have the balls to look at me, all he does is hang his head, as I shove the towel into his chest. Hard. "Fucking Jerk." I mutter to him, but I know that he's heard me. Loud and fucking clear. As I reach the end of the bar Jensen refuses to step aside, instead he stands in front of me, his feet a shoulders width apart, with his muscular tattooed arms folded across his very defined chest.

"Don't try and bullshit me, hot stuff. You walk out of here, you ain't ever coming back. You hear me?" Angry doesn't even come close to how I feel. If I were to slap this guy right now, right in his face, I highly doubt even that would calm me down. I can't believe this is happening to me. My heart is racing, my palms are clammy and I'm pissed that Joey hasn't even got my back on this. What a tool. I sure as hell know where his loyalties lie, the brown-nosing, two faced shit. Jensen doesn't say anything more to me. He just stands, watching me closely with his arms still crossed. Why does he have to be so good looking? I think that just makes me even more angry, and he's so smug about it too. Well if he thinks I'm going to bow down and play, then he's got another thing coming. No matter how hot he is.

"Move out of my way." I spit, unable to look him in the eyes, knowing that if I do, I will either slap him or say something that will get me fired. Neither of which, I want. He still doesn't say a thing, he just laughs and slowly moves to the side to let me pass, and gives my arse a light tap for good measure. I turn around and glare at him, but this does nothing other than heighten his amusement.

I step outside and light a cigarette. I know that I can't walk out of this job. It's all I've got while I'm here. I've got a course and bills that needed paying for, and I don't want to give that prick the satisfaction of knowing that he's affected me so much. I need a breather, that's all. If I can get through tonight without bumping into him, I'm sure I'll be fine. I've had way too much thrown on me in such a short space of time, that I don't know whether I'm coming or going. One thing that I do know, is that working with him is going to be an issue. He has that whole bad boy image down to a tee and I can't stand it. Holly should have known better, and really thought about it before handing temptation over to someone like him. She knows what I've been through. Fucking hell, and there's me thinking that I was the crazy one in the family. I check my phone again out of habit, but I know they can't find me here; at least I hope they can't anyway. I've changed my number anyway, what more can I do? Relief floods through me once again, when I'm greeted with a blank screen. A few months ago, I thought moving away would solve all of my problems, not make them worse.

"I thought you could do with this?" I raise my eyes from the invoices that are laid out before me, and strong, muscular tattooed arms grace my vision. As my eyes slowly trail upwards, they linger a little too long on his perfectly toned chest, clearly visible through his t-shirt with each breath he takes. If he was some old guy, maybe I would be able to deal with his shit in a better way, but when you've got a rugged, damaged angel stood in front of you, it's hard not stare.

"Fuck you." I snap, annoyed at myself for finding this guy attractive, and annoyed because I'm letting him get to me. Why has he even come back here anyway? To taunt me, or order me about some more?

"Fair enough, you don't have to like me. Fuck if I like that shitty little attitude you've got going on, but I expect nothing but respect while you're here working for *me.* You got that?"

I decide not to respond to him or his demands. Bloody hell, I've been there, I've done that and it's not a path I plan on taking again, anytime soon. Instead I stay silent while I take him in. I'd be lying if I said he wasn't attractive. Every goddamn thing about him is attractive. At roughly 6ft 3, his body is proportioned well. He's either an athlete of some sort, or he trains; hard. He's well built with massive broad shoulders and bulging biceps. I notice on his right arm, that he has a full sleeve of tattoos, but the light in the office isn't bright enough to allow me to see all of the details that are hiding within it. I have to fight the urge to lean over and touch it, to try and get a better look. His face, even with the scowl that is present every time he looks at me, is a face of rugged beauty, perfectly framed with day old stubble. His eyes, which automatically draw me in, are a deep dark brown and they are framed with dark long lashes. His lips are a deep red and perfectly plump and I can't help but wonder what they would feel like brushing next to mine. Finally, once I have soaked him up, I allow myself to speak.

"Where's Holly?"

"That, I can't tell you." Jensen says, as he steps closer to me and my body automatically stiffens as he steps way into my comfort zone, yet all he does is smile a little at my discomfort. "I bought the joint, that's all. It's nothing personal, so my bad if it's offended you. I don't know what else you want me to say, and I don't think there is anything else that I can say to help you. Now, you gonna get this down you or what? I need you out there, not in here. Plus one thing you need to know about me, is that I don't do idle chit chat either. You work, I pay. It's pretty simple."

"I'm good. I'd rather stay in here. I've got some paperwork that I need to catch up on anyway." I point to the mass of invoices laid out before me, hoping he'll take the hint. He doesn't and he's on me in seconds. His hands are firmly placed on either side of my chair as he leans over me, and my heart rate picks up quite quickly. He's that close, that I can feel the heat of his breath tickling my face.

"I pay you to be behind that bar, not to be sat in here on that fine arse of yours, hiding away."

"Who says I'm hiding? And just so you know, I'll do what the hell I want, when I want, *you hear me*?" I mimic him and I can tell instantly that he doesn't like it one little bit.

"Your eyes tell me a thousand tales sweetheart, but for now you'll do as I say. I told you before, this is my joint now and if you want to keep your job, you'll work for it."

Wow. What a control freak. I'd love nothing more than to pick up a large heavy object right now and throw it at his smart arsed face, but I know that violence only leads to further trouble and doesn't really solve anything. He doesn't move away while I continue to stare at him. Even with his face this uncomfortably close to mine, there is no way that I'm giving him the satisfaction of backing down.

"The bars filling up pretty fast out here... Whoa, sorry man." Joey cuts off as he notices us close together over in the corner. I'm pretty sure I can take a guess at what we must look like, yet Jensen doesn't pull away from me, he just cocks his head to the side and says, "Well what the fuck are you doing back here then?"

"I was..." He starts, but thinks better of it and mutters "never mind." as he quickly leaves the office. Jensen turns his attention back to me almost instantly and I'm greeted with a roguish grin, a grin that tells me I need to be very careful when I'm around him, or someone will get hurt. He's one of those guys that I'd swore to stay away from when I moved out here.

"Until next time, hot stuff." He leans in closer to me, and my breathing stops, unsure of what he's going to do and then slowly, he peels himself away from me.

"Keep wishing." I say, although it comes out much quieter than intended as I find myself short of breath. I can't believe this bell end is having this much of an effect on me. How can you hate someone, but want to know more about them at the same time? My head is well and truly done in.

Jensen steers clear of me for the rest of my shift and I don't know whether to be thankful or not. How long he's actually going to be staying around for is anyone's guess, but I hope he decides to leave sooner rather than later, for my sake as much as his. We've already clashed more times than I'm comfortable with and I feel weird whenever I'm around him. I need to get hold of Holly as soon as possible. Not only does she need to come back and sort all the crap out that she has left herself in, but she also needs to get this hunk of a man out of my life.

JENSEN

Another town, another joint. I've got no idea how long I'm going to be here for, but I'm here now and there's not much that I can really do about it, except make the most out of it that I can. I guess it's something new, a bit of a challenge and that's what I need right now. *A perfect distraction.* I'll only be here for a few months tops, anyway so I don't really need to familiarise myself with anything. With everyone occupied, I decide to take a full tour of Temptation without being interrupted. I'm not feeling the layout much and a lick of paint never hurt anyone, so that shouldn't be too much to sort out. Plus, if I get this place looking decent, I should be able to make a nice little profit when the time comes to sell up.

I thought the chick that owned this joint was having me on when she said I could buy it for such a bargain price. If I'm honest, I was expecting a major shit hole, but to be fair it's all right. The customers seem like regulars and that's always good for the cash flow. The staff on the other hand seem like they'll be a little bit harder to handle. That Joey kid looks out of his mind most of the time and to be honest, I'm not sure whether it's alcohol that he's on or something a little stronger. As long as he doesn't start making a dent in my profits, then all's good. That Anna chicks some piece of work though. Sexy, hell yes, she's fucking hot, but she's got her attitude all wrong. The sooner she shows me some respect and acts like she wants to be here, then the sooner she'll see that I'm a pretty decent guy to work for. Until then, if she wants me to make life hard for her, then she's in luck as that's my speciality.

Looking around the office, I notice that it could do with some major organisation too. Files and boxes are scattered around all over the goddamn place and nothing really seems to have a place of its own. Looks like that's going to be the first thing to be changed around here. Maybe I could get that Anna chick to do it seeing as she likes to be in here so much. I don't know what it is about her but she gets underneath my skin so bad. I feel so fucking uncomfortable in her presence, a feeling that I'm not familiar with and one that I don't want to be around. No matter what I do, I can't get her image out of my mind, the way she looked at me while I leaned down on top of here in that chair. Her eyes had a sexual longing in them, mixed with pure distaste and that alone caused all kinds of crazy shit to me. That smart mouth of hers drives me crazy and all I want to do is take her over my knee and punish her until she learns some goddamn respect. Fucking hell, I feel myself stir below at the mere thought of her underneath me, as I press myself into her. In a place like this, it shouldn't be too hard to find some willing chick to give me a distraction to easily fill my needs and after the day I've had, I'm going to fucking need it.

I look over to the bar as I lock up the office. Everyone seems to be having a good time, everyone except Anna. I don't know what her problem is and I don't think I want to find out either. I don't think I've even witnessed her smile yet. Jeez, she's one chick who needs to lighten up and fast. Maybe she just needs to get laid. With an attitude like hers, her boyfriend mustn't be satisfying her the way she needs.

"Why don't you get off for the night? Me and Joey have got this place under control, ain't that right Joe?" I say, giving him a nudge to the side as I step behind the bar, hoping he'll take the hint.

"Yeah, sure thing. We got it covered, Anna."

"I don't like this one fucking bit." She spits at me. "As soon as I get through to Holly, you're gone pal. I'd make the most of it if I were you, while you still can." She looks cute as hell as her nose wriggles while laying into me. No way, no way in hell would I allow some chick to talk to me like that, but this Anna chick, she's shit hot when she's angry and it's fucking good to watch. Plus, the angrier that she gets, the more entertaining she's becoming.

ANNA

I'm rudely awoken to the sounds of Pharell Williams, as my phone dances across my bedside unit beside me. I can barely open my eyes and I have no choice but to go in blind, whacking my hand on the unit during the process to try and find it, to stop the goddamn thing from ringing.

"Hello..." I say as I sleepily hold the phone to my ear.

"Anna, it's me..."

"Where the fuck are you?" I shout, cutting her off mid-sentence, suddenly wide awake as I shoot bolt upright in bed. "Why the hell haven't you been returning my calls?"

"I tried to call numerous times Anna, but the signal here's really shit. What's wrong? Why do you sound so worked up?" She asks. Did I actually just hear that right, or am I still dreaming? Why do I sound so fucking worked up? Shit, she's killing me here, really she is.

"You upped and left in the middle of the night without a seconds thought about anyone else. Not to mention the fact that you left me here to deal with your crap. Forgive me if you think that I'm a little worked up. I've got my own issues to work through and you know it." I scream at her. "You've got final fucking demands coming out of your arse, left, right and bloody centre and you've sold Temptation to an absolute bell end. What the hell has gotten into you recently?"

"Oh, so you've met Jensen then? He's pretty hot right?"

"No Holly, he's an arrogant, obnoxious, self-centred twat and you better tell him that you've changed your mind ASAP, or better still, get back here and deal with your shit yourself." Pretty hot, he maybe, but I'm not agreeing with her on this one. She's fucked up and she's fucked up big time. The sooner she realises this, the better. *For everyone's* sake.

"No can do, sweetie... Going, but... I'll..." The phone breaks up and then the line goes dead. I can't believe it. I have never felt so angry in all my life, like I have this past week. What the hell have I set myself up for by moving here?

I spend a short while looking at my phone

willing it to ring, but nothing happens. It doesn't help that I can't get Jensen out of my head either. All I can see is his face as he leans over me, while I secretly will him to do bad, bad things to me. I've never met someone who riles me up so much, so quickly, and now I'm most likely going to be spending most of my days with him and there's not a goddamn thing I can do about it.

Today is the day that I try to put an end to my stress and my anxiety. It's not guaranteed to work, but anything's worth a shot right now. I'm fed up of living my life in fear and worrying about the worst in everything. First things first. I really need to knuckle down on this assignment and start getting it together, ready to be handed in on time if I have any chance of passing it. If not, then I'm definitely going to be thrown off the course. I've had extensions, upon extensions and my tutor isn't going to take any more bullshit excuses from me. She said as much when I saw her last week. My head is that crammed with Temptation and the hot, obnoxious male that's suddenly rocked up into my life. Not to mention Holly and her sudden childish ways, that I don't even hear the front door open.

"It would seem that I just can't keep away." My head instantly snaps up at the sound of that voice. What the hell? Jensen stands before me looking all broody and dangerous; and mighty fine too. His hip is cocked to one side as he leans against the kitchen counter, staring right at me. I don't know how long he's been stood here watching me, but I suddenly feel uncomfortable in my own home.

"What..." I swallow hard, unsure if I can get the words to leave my lips. "What the fuck are you doing here? Are you stalking me or something now?"

"I wouldn't flatter yourself, sweetheart. You might be hot, but not enough to risk jail for."

"So why are you here?" I demand.

"Because I can be. I guess I could ask you the same thing." The smile on his face is the arrogant one that I have very quickly become accustomed to.

"Surely you're not that stupid? Obviously, it's pretty clear that I live here." I signal the surroundings before me, as if to prove a point. "How about you do yourself a favour and go before I call the cops?"

"Why would I want to do that?" He slowly steps towards the old antique coffee table where I'm currently seated, pens and paper scattered everywhere, and he leans in and grabs the chair next to me. He spins it around and sits facing me, so that his chest is pressed against the back-rest, all the while he never breaks eye contact with me. An image of me straddling him, the way he's straddling that chair flickers in my mind and I feel like slapping myself for allowing that thought build up in my mind. Not only has this intruder taken residence of my bar, but he has now somehow found himself positioned in my kitchen without my permission. "Maybe you should call the cops, it'd be pretty funny to watch, actually."

"Why would you even want to spend your time here? Surely you have much more *exciting* things that you could be doing? I don't know, like pissing someone else off?"

"Normally I'd say that you were right, but seeing as though I'm new in town, it's only fair that I check out my humble abode. It's not really my style, but I guess it'll have to do."

Wow, this guy's really taking the piss. The sooner he hops up out if that chair and out of my life the better. Why am I even letting him get to me like this?" "Very funny, Jensen. As you can see, I've got some pretty important stuff that needs my attention. If you want to see me that much, then you've got my whole shift later." Why did I just say that? I don't want to encourage this arsehole, but if it gets him out of my way then so be it.

"Do I look like I'm being funny?" He snarls and I take in his serious face, gone is the bad boy smirk, instead now he has a fierce scowl present on his ruggedly beautiful features. No. Sitting here right in this moment, I don't think he's being funny for a second. Yesterday comes flashing back to the forefront of my memory. Two suited and booted men standing at my door wanting to talk to me, and then the card. Shit, the letting agency.

"Oh my god." I say out loud. "Holly's sold this place too, and she's fucking sold it to you?"

"Got it in one. Who knew beneath that pretty face of yours, that you could be such a bright spark?" His cocky and oh, so sure of himself grin is back in full force.

"You do realise that you can't actually buy this place don't you?"

"And why's that?" His eyebrow's shoot up and a questioning scowl forms as he looks directly at me. I don't know whether to laugh, or cry, or do both from the mixed emotions that are taking assault on my body.

"Because I fucking live here, goddamnit. You can't possibly expect to just turn up here and boot me out of my own home." Panic begins to set in as the crap that Holly has left me in starts to form into reality before my very own eyes.

"Really? You'd like to think so, huh? Fortunately for you, I'm not as much of a bastard as you seem to think. Plus like I said, you're a bit of all right to look at. I guess I could get used to seeing you every now and again. Maybe I'll let you stay, but only if you're prepared to play nice."

"Maybe you'll let me?" I say as he stands up and leans over me. My breath catches and my heart rate picks up at the close proximity between us as he moves in closer to me. My whole body is turning against me and he knows it.

As his mouth reaches my ear, he bends even closer to me and whispers, "think of all the things that I could do to you. Knowing that I am this close to you, and knowing that you want me just as much, has me so fucking hard right now." His finger slowly brushes along my jawline, until he finds my lips and gently traces the outline, which in turn causes an eruption of sensations to explode within my core. "I can't wait to feel these perfect lips around me. I bet you'd feel so fucking good."

My hand connects with his face before I even realise what I'm doing and a sharp sting is left in its wake. His beautiful, deep dark brown eyes hood over and he looks completely feral, if only for a few seconds before his face falls into a relaxed state and then he laughs a little before backing away.

"Don't forget to have my dinner on the table for when I'm back, honey." He throws me a wink, before he turns on his heels and makes his way back to the front door. All the while, I'm sat here, completely speechless at the events that have just taken place. What an arrogant son of a bitch. I want to slap him so fucking hard, but at the same time I can't help the feeling of excitement that dances within me at the prospect of waking up to that delicious sight every single day.

I spend more time than usual getting ready for my shift than I normally would. I make sure that I spend more time with my hair and I actually do something with it, rather than just pinning it back. I also pay more attention to my eye make-up too and I can't help but mentally kick myself for it. I'm so confused right now. I don't like him, but I want him to notice me. I feel uncomfortable with him around, yet I feel alive. He makes me so angry when I see him, but he also makes me want to do bad, bad things to him. Bollocks. He's the type of guy I need to stay away from, but something about him draws me in, yet at the same time I can't stand the goddamn sight of him. Finally, once I'm happy with my appearance for the evening, I pull my door open and make my way across the narrow landing. Stood straight in my line of vision is Jensen. I try to avert my eyes as he walks towards me, fresh out of the shower in just a towel, which is only just about closed loosely around his waist. One sudden movement and all his manhood would be on show. As he nears closer to me, the tiny droplets of water on his body become visible, and the look in his eyes has me shivering from head to toe. He looks like a lion ready to strike.

"Like something you see, Anna?" A smirk curves his face as he watches my discomfort and the need to slap him resurfaces. He's so pissing sure of himself, and it drives me crazy. Yes, I may be fighting the urge to reach out and touch him, to feel those strong, hard, tattooed biceps for myself, but he doesn't need to know that. I swallow hard, trying to lubricate my mouth as it's dry as hell. "Nothing to say?" He goads me further. "Normally that smart mouth of yours is running ten to the dozen, right about now."

I don't reply, instead I just stand here like

a misplaced piece of furniture. I notice that his cheek still bears the imprint of my hand from when I slapped him earlier and it fills me with a weird feeling of satisfaction. Still, even my silence doesn't stop him in his pursuit as he gets even closer to me, as I continue to stand motionless outside my bedroom door. His hands reach up and rest above my head on either side of the doorframe, blocking me in as he looks down at me.

"Meeting anyone nice tonight?" He asks.

"I don't think that's any of your business."

"To hell it is, if it's on my watch."

"I didn't realise you were moving in so soon." I say, trying for a different approach.

"I don't waste time Anna. Ever. You need to learn that about me pretty quick." His eyes never leave me, as his forehead rests against mine and I can't stop my heart from thudding in a desperate attempt to break free out of my rib cage, yet at the same time I feel uneasy about him being this close to me.

"If you don't mind, I've got to leave soon. I wouldn't want to turn up late for my shift, would I?" I smile at him through gritted teeth and he knows he's having this effect on me.

"No worries. Anna, you're looking pretty good by the way. Who knows, maybe later I might just show you what a real man can do."

My sudden sharp intake of breath is audible and for the second time today, Jensen pulls away from me laughing as he turns on his heels to head in the opposite direction. Fucking prick.

"Get your act together woman. You've experienced men like him before and we all know how that ended." I think to myself. *"You need to get over whatever it is that you're feeling when you're around him, because no fucking good can come of this."*

JENSEN

I had no fucking idea that I would find Anna in my new place when I arrived here. I guess I should have put two and two together sooner, but maths was never really my strong point. Of course, it makes sense that she would live here, seeing as though I bought the joint from her cousin and those two practically seem to do everything together.

As I pulled up in the driveway of my new humble abode, I thought I'd check the exterior first before heading inside. I won't lie; it's a nice little house. Cosy, even. It's a detached with a little garden and it's pretty oldy-worldy too, but who gives a shit? It may not be something that I would have picked out myself, but seeing as though it was thrown into the deal, there's no way I could have refused. Who doesn't love a little investment every now and again, plus I'll probably only be around for a few months max anyways. Every single place that I have ever lived, and that's been a whole lot of places; they've always been temporary and I can't see any reason why this place is going to be any different.

That's when I see her. That crazy arse, smart mouth chick from Temptation last night. I stand transfixed on the spot and watch her for a moment. She's lost in thought, frantically scribbling over bits of paper that are scattered out before her. Her blonde hair falls in waves and rests at the peak of her breasts and her heart shaped face is set at an angle; pen poised at her lips as she ponders whatever is going through her mind. I continue to stand and watch her as she draws me, in while debating whether or not I should knock before I enter. Fuck that. It's my house after all, and if needs be I'll just use my key. It's not like I'll be trespassing on my own property, is it?

Now, here I am, finding myself pressed up against her door in nothing but a towel and I can't help but feel smug at knowing that she hates me, but also wants to fuck me with a passion. Women, they're all the fucking same. It's not hard to see that I intimidate her, but I know she's curious as hell to find out more about me and it will only be a matter of time no doubt, before she gives in. Sooner, now that we're practically roomies.

My dick stirs to life as I lean in closer to her. The moment her breath hitches, I know that I have her exactly where I want her. Sweet, sweet, victory dances from my lips on a laugh and I walk away from her knowing that she's left wanting so much more. The image of her is still at the forefront of my mind. Her outfit was a little bit tighter than last night and her eyes a little darker. Fuck me, she's hot. I have to push myself down to relieve the pressure, while wishing it was someone else's hand, or mouth entirely. Where the hell is Darcie at when I need her? Maybe it's about time I gave her a long, overdue call.

"Boyd, get the fuck in here man. What took you so long? Get a move on, it's pissing it down out here."

"I'm coming. Chill the fuck out. What's with the rush anyways?" He shouts back.

"New neighbourhood. You know how it is. I haven't worked out how nosey the neighbours are yet." I say, looking straight at my main man. Boyd soon comes crashing through the door with heaps of boxes from his car.

"You gonna tell me what's in here or what? These little shits weigh a ton."

"Ask no questions, be told no lies my friend. You know the rules." I reply, while patting him on the shoulder as he passes through. Even if I did tell him, it would be nowhere near as interesting as the suspense that's now flowing through his overactive mind, so I leave it at that and say no more.

"Well that's all that got dropped. You want me to call if anymore arrive?"

"Damn straight. Hey, you heading straight back, or you fancy checking this new joint of mine out?" I get the feeling that Boyd's in no rush to head back and it'll be good to catch up with him. It's been a crazy arse few weeks and I've not had any time with my wingman in a while.

"You really need to ask me? Bars equal hot chicks man, and hot chicks make Boyd a happy guy." He dives through the door with a knowing goofy smile plastered on his face, as he shakes off the excess water from the rain. Always the fucking playboy. I bet Anna would have had a major fucking hissy fit if she'd been at home. She's so fucking uptight it's unreal. I've never met a chick like her, and its blowing my fucking mind. I can't help but wonder when she last got laid. Maybe I could help her with that; help her relieve some of that pent up frustration that she holds in so well.

I met Boyd a good few years back. He was in knee deep just as much as me, with no one around who was willing to give him another chance. It was us two against the world and it still is to this very day. The only thing is, I move around a lot, but Boyd; he's practically my mother fucking furniture. Wherever I go, he goes.

"It's a pretty neat place man." He says as he looks around the bar. "How long you planning on staying for?"

"Who knows? It could be a month, maybe two. I'm not sure; who knows, maybe this place could grow on me." My eyes land on Anna as the words leave my mouth. I don't know what it is, but something about her has me wanting more, but fuck if that attitude of hers grates on my balls. My eyes remain fixed on her until she senses me watching and I call her over. Her body snakes towards us, her midriff slightly on show and I feel myself stir again just from looking at her. I can't help but laugh to myself, as she looks at me with hooded eyes, yet her jaw is set tight with a perfect scowl across her face for everyone in the goddamn bar to see.

"How about a service with a smile?" I can't help but goad her.

"What can I get you?" She asks but her face remains the same. Un-fucking-believable.

"We'll take two doubles of whatever takes your fancy and get them over here ASAP."

"Hot damn. Who's the chick man? You reckon you could hit me up?" Boyd says, as his tongue is practically hanging from his mouth.

"Not a fucking chance. That one, she's a no-go, you hear me?"

"Loud and clear boss, loud and fucking clear."

ANNA

What a jerk. How dare he come in here and speak to me like he owns me. How dare he make me look stupid for his own fucking enjoyment? There is no way that I'm going to be spoken to like that from anybody, least of all Jensen. I angrily pour two shots of jack into some glasses and pour some beer over them before I add a slice of lime to each drink.

"You okay?" Joey is soon by my side looking all frantic as he senses the tension that is rolling from me.

"Ah, I will be Joe. I wouldn't worry too much about me. You see that smart arse over there? Let me tell you something. He's a fucking prick and the sooner he's out of my life the fucking better."

"Shit Anna, I've never seen you hate on someone so much before. It kind of makes me think I'm in with a chance here, girl." His hand cups my arse as he moves in closer to me, making me feel instantly on edge.

"Don't push your luck buddy." I swat his hand away, while trying to keep my cool, when all I want to do is slap him across the face for getting up in my comfort zone. Anyone ever heard of respect around here? Jeez, this place really is starting to crawl with 'em. "Keep your hands to yourself too, okay?" I pick up the tray and set off to give Mr Smart arse and his pal their drinks. A wicked smile creeps onto his lips as soon as he spots me getting closer, and I smile back in the sweetest way possible which causes him to falter slightly.

"Here we are boys." I say as I pass a beer to Jensen's pal, ensuring that I give them the smile that Jensen is after.

"That's a good girl." Jensen laughs and I quickly turn to face him. He holds his hand out for his beer and I don't think twice as I lift it high and pour it over his head.

"That's me done for the night, sir." I smile and a crowd close to us start to whoop and cheer, while Jensen is sporting a furious look on his face. "See you around." I shout out to his buddy before turning around and walking out of Temptation without a backwards glance and my head firmly held high.

"Fuck!" I shout louder than intended to and a few passers-by stop to look my way. Next time that I decide to dress fucking sexy, maybe I'll check the weather. The rain is pouring down and within seconds my top clings to my chest, not exactly hiding the girls either. All I want to do is get home and get in a steaming hot shower and wash the day away.

"Anna." Why did I think he wouldn't come after me? I've just poured his profits over his head, in front of his punters, not to mention his buddy. Of course he's going to come after me. From what I've gathered already, Jensen isn't the type of guy to take that shit lying down. "Anna, hold the fuck up."

I keep walking, eager to get away from him and the anger that he's making me feel. If my past has taught me anything, it's to walk the hell away from a bad situation. I pick my pace up and soon hear the thud of running feet behind me. Shit. He's really not going to let this go. Strong hands grip me from behind and I'm soon spun around to face him.

"What the fuck was that?" He asks while searching my face, as if by just looking at me he'll get my answer. His deep dark browns look livid, but I couldn't care less. No way will I let anyone speak to me as if I am below them. I may be his *employee* now, but I'm still fucking human. "Answer me, goddamnit. What's your fucking problem?"

"You!" I shout. "You're my fucking problem. Can you not see that? Everywhere I go, you're there. I have to work with you and on top of that I now also have to live with you, not to mention having to listen to you speaking to me like shit whenever you get the chance."

"Well you know where the door is. If you don't like it, that ain't my problem. You don't have to stay. I'm being pretty goddamn reasonable letting you stay, don't you think?"

"You just don't get it do you? You're a prick. I want you to back out if this *arrangement* that you and Holly have come up with. That way you can leave me the hell alone." I'd never admit it to him, but his powerful stance over me has me wanting him more. I must be out of my mind.

"Here's some news for you. I do what I want, when I want. No one tells me what to do, okay? And this shitty little attitude of yours isn't going to get you very fucking far, lady."

"Go and find someone who is prepared to deal with your shit Jensen, because I'm done." The rain continues to pour down, his shirt almost like a second skin and again I find part of myself wanting to reach out, just to see how those muscles feel underneath my touch.

"If you're going to live with me, you're going to need to get used to a few things and fast."

"And if I don't...?" I start but he cuts me off.

"Then you go. It's as simple as that. I don't know you, you don't know me. Sure you might have a decent rack, but what good are you to me apart from being behind that bar and staying there?"

His hands are scrunched up in his jean pockets as he looks at me waiting for my answer, but the truth is, I actually have no answer to his question. "Haven't you got a bar that you need to get back to? Like I said before, I'm going home." A tiny, small part of me expects him to call after me, or pull me back. The scary thing is a part of me wants him to do just that, but he doesn't and the feeling that I am left with as I watch him walk away from me, is an unwelcome and uncomfortable one.

No matter how much I try, sleep doesn't want to come for me anytime soon. I've been lay in bed for the past three hours listening to my music, in the hope that it would help me to drift off. Yet here I am; wide-a-fucking-wake. I remove my earplugs and the house seems quiet. I guess Jensen isn't back yet; or maybe he won't bother coming back here tonight at all. Here's hoping. I pull myself up and throw on an overly large t-shirt and head downstairs to grab a drink. I'm still nervous about being home alone, but the thought of Jensen appearing at any moment kind of keeps my anxiety at bay. All the lights are out downstairs, so he definitely hasn't come back yet, which is a relief in a way. I really wish Holly would come back soon. Maybe then we will finally be able to sort this out, once and for all.

Switching on the light, I step towards the refrigerator and pull out the milk. When I was little, I always used to sneak downstairs to grab a glass of milk in the middle of the night. I guess it's kind of my comforter.

"Now, I could definitely get used to seeing you like this."

"What the..." I spin around and I'm instantly greeted by a shirtless Jensen sitting in front of me, at the large antique table. "Why are you sat in the dark?" The question involuntarily falls from my lips. I didn't have any inclination to make small talk with him, yet here I am surprising myself when it comes to him once again. He doesn't answer me; instead he continues to sit there, slowly undressing me with his eyes. I clear my throat and ask, "do you want a drink?"

"Nah, I'm good." He rolls a tumbler of golden liquid in the palm of his hands. "What's your deal Anna?" Now it's my turn to refuse to answer him. When I left Temptation earlier, I didn't envisage small talk in the kitchen.

"No deal." I finally say, but my voice doesn't sound as confident as I would like it to.

"When did you last get laid?" His tone is flat and all matter of fact, as if he's arranging a business transaction, not something personal.

"That's really none of your goddamn business is it?" I snap, and he instantly has my back up. Well we managed a conversation for a couple of seconds before it turned shitty. Some would say that was progress.

"I'm making it my business. You're so uptight, so on edge all of the time. It's not right. No one should have to act like that." His eyes never leave mine, not for a second, and I'm feeling slightly uncomfortable in his presence. I feel like he can see into the depths of my soul. I feel as though he can see my past flashing across his eyes and he's just waiting for me to stand here and admit it.

"You know shit about me, so don't sit there and try to judge me on what you think you know."

As soon as those words leave my mouth, he's on me in an instant and I find myself pinned against the refrigerator with nowhere to go. I'm utterly speechless as I look up at him. The power that emanates from him has my breathing in a frenzy.

"I've got an idea. How about we try and get along. Who knows, we might even get to have a little fun along the way? That's only if you like fun. Tell me, do you like having a little fun Anna?" He must assume my silence as agreement to his question, as his lips slowly lower down onto mine. He tastes me gently for a few moments, before seeking hungrily for more with his tongue. I'm frozen in place as I allow him to explore and my head is dizzy from the intoxication of his presence. My whole body comes to life as his hard, solid body presses close against mine, only the thin material of my battered, overly large, t-shirt coming between us. My hands find their way to his muscular, tattooed chest and I finally feel those muscles beneath my palms. Something that I have been secretly wanting to do since I first laid my eyes on him, and he feels better than I ever imagined. Finally after a few more moments of relishing in the way he's making me feel, I push him away and it's much harder to do, than I initially thought.

"This isn't going to happen. It can't happen." I whisper and I don't think even I believe what I'm saying. He smiles his wicked smile and pulls back to let me pass and gives me a firm slap in the arse, as I walk away. The sharp sting that is left behind has me even more desperate for him and all I want to do is kick myself, again and again. *Anna Jameson, where the hell has your willpower and determination gone?*

"Any sign of when you're coming back?" I'm propped up on the counter, phone in one hand and a mug of coffee in the other, while trying to coax Holly into giving me some information on her wayward plans. Jensen chooses this moment to come strolling into the kitchen in nothing but his boxers. The sight of him in almost all of his glory, causes my mind to wander to places that I don't want it to go. "Just make sure you hurry that arse up and get back here. I couldn't give a rat's arse about Hernandez, it's more about going behind my back. Not just with the bar, but with the house too..."

"Anna, quit moaning. Relax a little and you'll see that Jensen's an all right guy. Just get to know him a little bit and you'll soon see." I can't help myself and I burst out laughing at her statement.

"Are we talking about the same guy here? Were you high or some shit when you spoke to him? He's the biggest prick I've ever had the displeasure of meeting." I say while looking directly at him as he pulls a chair out in front of me. He must know that I'm talking about him, as he holds his hand over his chest to feign his hurt and laughs. It's a cute laugh and his whole face changes, he looks younger and carefree somehow and I wouldn't mind getting to know that side of him. Instead, I have to deal with the arrogant, obnoxious arsehole that appeared in my bar a few nights back. I say a quick goodbye to Holly and let her go, after I've made it perfectly clear that this isn't over with.

"How do?" He nods in my direction. His morning voice is croaky from sleep and his hair is a beautiful ruffled mess.

"Piss off." Is all I manage, before jumping down from the counter.

"Hey, I thought we were being nice and giving friends a go?"

"I thought I told you to piss off?" He looks slightly taken aback as the words that I have said register in his head. I'd be lying to myself if I said the sight of him first thing in a morning didn't send chills of pleasure running through my body. God I'm so confused right now. The guys a jerk and I shouldn't be wasting my time thinking about him, but seeing him, sat here in all his glory, it's enough to give any woman a mental breakdown.

JENSEN

"This chick is gonna be nothing but trouble." I think to myself. I've never had anyone act that way towards me before. Women, they've always been easy for me, but Anna? Not a fucking chance. Shit, her holding back, going hot to cold, has me wanting her like crazy. I want to get to know her, find out what makes her tick, but her attitude fucking stinks. No wonder she seems fucking lonely, she probably has next to no friends. Other than that Holly chick, anyway. Last night, I really thought she'd give in, finally cave, and let go of whatever it is that's making her hold back and be so uptight. I guess I thought she'd stop being a bitch, but there sure ain't no sign of that happening any time soon.

She should be thanking her lucky fucking stars that she isn't out on her arse. Anyone else would be, but she's a chick and I just can't do it. Plus, there's just something about her that leaves me high and dry and wanting more.

"You comin' or what?"

"Yeah, yeah. Just give me a sec man." I've spent the morning trying to get all my shit into this tiny house and it's taken me much longer than I thought it would do, and now I've got Boyd howling at me to get a move on.

"Why don't you just get someone to move it for you?" He asks.

"Because no one touches my stuff. I'll put it all in here." I say, as I point to the living area. I'm a private guy and anyone touches my shit, then they're likely to lose movement of their fingers and he knows it too. "You gonna just stand there, or are you gonna give me a hand carting these boxes around?"

"Listen bud, if we don't leave now, then we ain't gonna get there on time. Just put it all to one side and do it later. What harm can it do?"

Finally admitting defeat and checking the time, I realise that he's right. The traffic around here is an absolute joke and this is something that I can't be late for. On a sigh, I pull the last box into the living area and head for the door. "Looks like you're gonna need to put those club feet down and pronto. I ain't waiting another month or so to see him."

"You got it man. You better hold on tight."

After a couple of hour's drive and having to listen to Boyd's shit taste in music, we finally arrive at our destination. It's not somewhere that I particularly enjoy travelling to, but it's got to be done. Loyalty is one thing and family is something else altogether. No matter what shit's gone down in the past, for Mitchell, I'll always be here. I wonder how he'll act when he sees me. I wonder if he's still pissed as hell at me. We haven't spoken since before he ended up back here and the last time I saw him, he wasn't in a good place either. So when I got his letter, I knew I couldn't pass up the opportunity to see him again. I'm just anxious as to what he's going to say. The guy's head is all over the place and you never know if it's Mitchell that's going to greet you or his psychotic twin.

I see him instantly, sat brooding at the table with his arms crossed over his chest. His fearful frown is visible from the other side of the room. To look at him, you'd think he was fucking scary and feel the need to stay away, and you wouldn't be far wrong. As long as you're honest with him and treat him with respect, he's your best friend and will do anything for you. But get on his bad side and Mitchell Blake isn't someone you want to cross, unless you've got a death wish. Growing up around him gave me some major positives, like respect and never needing to go without, but it also came with the negatives too. I never knew if he'd be coming home, or if someone was going to boot the door down. I looked up to Mitchell like his was a god. I didn't know any different. He could do no wrong in my eyes, but as I grew and the older I became, I realised that I didn't want that sort of lifestyle anymore. That was my life back then, and I believe I'm a stronger person because of it. I also know that whatever Mitchell did, he did it to protect me from an early age. Now, I much prefer to keep my head down and travel to somewhere new as soon as things begin to get predictable.

"Look at you, looking all respectable." I look down at my black t-shirt, black jeans and battered black boots and realise some things never change.

"How do. You're looking pretty good man." I say, and I mean it.

"Well what else do you think I can do all day, sit on my arse and drive myself crazy? So, tell me, you okay? No one giving you any trouble?" He asks, his face set serious, with his fists clenching in front of him on the small white table.

"I'm good. I can't complain. I get about, you know how it is. Never stay in the same place for too long. What about you? I didn't expect to hear from you after last time..." I say, but he cuts me off.

"Fuck last time. You're my little brother and if I call you, you come. Or has that suddenly changed?"

"You bein' serious? You know I'd come for you anytime you asked. I guess I didn't think you'd want to see me, that's all." I say, getting more pissed at him the longer I sit here.

"Well, shits changing. I'll be home sooner than I thought, so I'm gonna need somewhere to stay while I get myself together."

"That won't be a problem. You can stay with me, but I don't want none of your shit following you, you hear me? I'm done with that crap now, Mitchell." The last thing I need right now is Mitchell bringing his crap to my door when Anna's there. I don't know why I'm bothered about what Anna thinks, but for some reason I am. I want to make sure she's safe, and that nothing from our pasts can come back and hurt her. Shit, this chicks really gotten under my skin.

"Little brother, I'm done too. The only reason that I'm here is a bad case of *wrong place, wrong time.*"

"What about Dominic?" I swear to god that joke better not be floating around.

"Nah, forget Dominic, you don't need to worry about him. He won't be around for a very long time. Plus he has no issues with you. I think his problem is that chick he was with. He's still pretty pissed that she didn't have his back. I can't remember her name, but she's better off away from him anyway. No woman should have to experience a jerk like him. I just hope she listened to my advice and moved the hell away from the area."

"Yeah, I guess. So what's the plan from here? Have you been given any dates or...?"

"Jensen, I know nothing. It's the safest way to play this. I sit and wait, that's all I can do and no one can start asking questions. Anyway, rumour has it that you've got yourself a new bar. Why don't you tell me about it?"

"That rumour would be true. It's pretty neat. It needs a lick of paint, but it's got some good potential, especially as an investment. Hey, maybe you could work for me when you're back? That way, I can keep an eye on your sorry arse?" Now that I would pay to see. Mitchell isn't one to do your usual regular nine to five jobs. He prefers something with more of a risk involved. He thrives off danger, always has and probably always will. One day, that will probably be the death of him.

"Who knows, maybe it'll be good for my soul and I might just be able to redeem myself. What d'ya say?" Sarcasm was never his strong point, but it makes me happy to see that he's taking an interest in my day to day business. It's been a lonely place without him.

Before I know it, my time is up and I'm soon being ushered out of the room. I don't know if I'll see him before he's home. I just hope that this time he keeps me in the fucking loop.

"I'll be in touch with the details, J." He shouts after me and I feel lighter somehow, now that I know the tension between us has been cleared. It looks like I might just get my brother back, and I don't know whether to be happy or worried about it with the shit that's bound to follow him.

ANNA

I've spent the whole of my morning rushing around and my heads been all over the place. I almost had to go back home, as I thought I'd left my assignments, only to find them stuffed into the side pocket of my bag. I seriously need to take some time out here and soon, otherwise I'm going to end up fucking up my future. A future that I'm trying to create for myself, while burning my arse into the ground. Everything seems to be going from bad to worse right now and I have no idea how to stop it. Maybe if I faced the fact that Holly isn't going to be returning home anytime soon, I might just be able to move on with my life a little. That doesn't help with the douche that's currently occupying my house though. Jensen is a completely different ball game and I'm definitely going to need a clear head to deal with him. Preferably not face to face, because that man erases all sense of control from me.

When I finally pull up outside college, it takes a few minutes for me to collect myself and to double check that I have everything that I need. Just as I'm about to exit the car, my phone chimes to life beside me. Instantly I feel panic begin to bubble inside my chest. *Calm down, answer it Anna.* I mentally chant to myself before plucking up enough courage to look at the screen. It's not a number I recognise. Shit, now what do I do? Maybe it's Holly calling from a different number. But what if it isn't? What if they've found me?

"Don't be so stupid." I mutter to my steering wheel. There's no way that they can find me here. No one knows that I have family here, so why would they suspect that this is where I'll be? My phone is still dancing in the palm of my hand as I continue to have my little meltdown. I guess I can always say it's a wrong number. Taking in a deep breath, I answer the phone and lift it slowly to my ear wearily, as if it might explode at any given moment.

"Hello." I say quietly down the speaker.

"Anna, honey. Is that you? How are you?" I feel and hear the audible sound of relief escape me, as I let go of my breath that I have been holding in. "Why haven't you called? I've been so worried about you."

"I've been busy, you know? I was gonna call real soon, I promise. It's just... There hasn't been enough time."

"You sure you're okay girl? You don't sound right, you sound off. You're not ill are you?"

"Honestly Dad, I'm fine. I just didn't expect you to call. Well, not after the last time we spoke anyway."

"You're my little girl and don't you ever forget that. We all say things that we don't mean when we're hurt and angry. You reckon you could find it in that beautiful heart of yours to forgive an old guy like me?" I instantly feel at ease and let out a shakey laugh. "Now that's my girl."

"Oh Dad, really there's nothing to forgive on this side. I should be saying that to you, after everything that I put you through. I didn't think that you'd want to speak to me again." The last time I spoke to my Dad was just as I was leaving for Holly's. My head was all over the place and I needed him to try and understand that I needed to leave, but he just wouldn't have any of it. All he would do was beg me to stay. Tell me that, no matter what had happened, we could get through it and everything would work out just fine. Looking into his eyes and telling him that I couldn't stand the thought of spending one more day with him, hurt me like hell. It was all I could do to make him think that I hated him so he would let me go. Make him think that all this, everything that I was going through, was because of him. To make him believe that I got mixed up in the wrong crowd, because he didn't care that mum just vanished, when all it really did was shatter what was left of my already broken heart.

"Dad..."

"Anna. It's okay. I know you didn't mean what you said. I've known you a pretty long time and I can tell when you're lying to me. I just need to know that you're okay? Really okay? Everything that was happening back then that made you leave, is it sorted now? I'd hate to think that you were in some kind of trouble, and you're out there on your own."

Well shit, how do I answer that? "I'm not sure Dad, but know that I'm safe here. I miss you like crazy you know and I hope that one day I can come back to see you, but it just doesn't feel like the right time just yet, you know?"

"Okay." He sighs down the line. God, I really miss him and just hearing his voice has my almost healed wounds opening again. "Well, call me when you can, and if you ever need me, you know where I am. Regardless of what it is, I'm always here for you."

"I know. Thanks Dad, and I really am sorry, for everything. I'll try and call you soon, I promise."

"I love you baby girl, no matter what has happened you'll always have me."

I allow the hot, salty, tears to fall down my face as I remain motionless in the car. I never expected to hear from him again. When I walked away from that life, I walked away from everything and everyone in it. I had to. I had no choice if I wanted to make sure that they remained safe. What the hell did I get myself into and why couldn't I see how serious it was?

"But I loved him." I say to myself. As long as I had *him*, he'd protect me from the stuff that was happening beyond my control. I loved him and I truly believed that he loved me too, but obviously that didn't do me any good did it? He clearly didn't love me like he said he did. Otherwise I wouldn't be in this fucking mess in the first place. All the progress that I have made begins to slowly unravel from the sound of my father's voice. I need to get strong, and fast. I haven't come this far to fall at the first goddamn hurdle.

"I'm so happy that you finished it this time around, Miss Jameson." My tutor looks up at me from behind her desk with a warm smile on her porcelain face. She holds a look of pure beauty and kindness and I can't help but feel comfortable in her presence. "It looks like you might just be back on track for this course. Keep it up and there'll be no problems."

"Thanks, Miss Tanner. I don't want to fall behind again so you can be sure that it won't happen again." I smile back at her.

"Now that's what I like to hear. Excuse me if you think that I am speaking out of turn, I apologise, but if you need support, then we have people here who may be able to help you. Pressure and anxiety can be quite common when it comes to your exams."

"I'm good, but thank you." I say, declining her offer politely. No way will I be sitting down with a counsellor to discuss my problems. Nothing they say will be able to help me. They definitely won't be able to make it go away. Not now, not ever. What good will talking do, anyway? I don't see how dragging up the past and reliving it for someone else to hear is going to help me. If anything, it will only make me worse, like going through it all over again. I like to keep my private life *private*, and that's how it's going to stay. I pick up my bag from the floor and say my goodbyes, desperate to make my escape. As I reach the door Miss Tanner stops me in my tacks.

"We are here for you, you know. We want to see you succeed, and I will do anything that I can to make that happen." All I can do is nod in her direction in thanks. The lump that has formed in my throat prevents me from talking. Why would she do that? I'm guessing there are other students on this course that could also do with some extra support, if not more than me. I'm immensely grateful that she cares, but the last thing I want, or need right now is special treatment. If I'm going to pass this, then I want to pass because I did it on my own merit, without any help from others.

The drive back home doesn't take too

long and the traffic that has been taking over the roads for the past few weeks, has backed off somewhat. Before I know it, I'm outside the house, when I suddenly find that I can't pull up onto my driveway because some dirty white truck is parked there. I swear to god, if this is Jensen playing one of his silly little games, then I'm going to ring his fucking neck. Admitting defeat, I kill the engine and block the truck in. Two can play that game. Until he learns to set some boundaries and play by the rules, then we're going to have a fucking problem.

"Jensen." I shout as I open the front door. "Jensen, you here?" The house seems quiet but that means nothing. He likes to hide out in the dark, so it wouldn't surprise me if he's just sitting somewhere like the kitchen.

"Fuck," I scream as I round the corner and whack my toe on something hard. I take in the sight before me and all I can see are boxes, heaps and heaps of boxes. Some are piled on top of each other and some are just scattered randomly, here, there and everywhere. What's going on? *Calm down Anna. Take a deep breath.* This shit is getting unreal. So he's moving his stuff in, that's fine. Would it have hurt to move it all out all out of the way first?

ANNA

"You're early."

"Me? What's up with you? Have you pissed the bed again, or something?" Seeing Joe in here on time, or even early is beginning to worry me a little. "What are you doing here?"

"Had to cover Jensen's shift, so here I am. Jeez, how do you do the day shifts in here? It's fucking dead."

"You work, you get paid Joe. It's not always about getting your leg over, you know. So why'd you have to cover his shift?" I ask as I stuff my bag behind the bar. I know that it's none of my business, but I'm a curious soul.

"What do you take me for? You think I'm gonna ask him to tell me what he's up to? He's my boss, Anna, and plus, I don't fancy chancing his temper."

"Yeah, you've got a point there. I'm gonna chance it though and I don't give a toss how he reacts either. I got home and all his shit was left lying around the house. Boxes are everywhere Joe and I don't think I can take it anymore. I almost broke my foot when I walked through the goddamn door."

"Trouble in paradise then, hot stuff?" He laughs and nudges me slightly, clearly trying to lighten the mood.

"Paradise, Jensen and I, is something that will never go into the same sentence. Ever." What planet is this guy on? "Speaking of which, has he showed his face yet?"

"Nah. He called me last night to see if I could cover. Who am I to deny the man that holds the power?"

"You fucking denied me left, right and centre, when I held the power."

"Hey hot stuff, I'll think you'll find that it's you who always denied me and my advances."

"Oh piss off Joe." I laugh, as I throw a towel in his direction. "Why don't you ever take anything I say seriously?"

"Because, there's no fun in that whatsoever." He says as I'm once again patted on the arse.

"If you value your balls, you won't do that again."

"Oh, I love it when you talk dirty to me."

"If you two want to fuck, how about you

take it elsewhere, instead of in my bar?"

I don't need to turn around to know who that voice belongs to. Automatically my senses are on high alert. When I do turn around, I begin to wish I hadn't. His face is livid and his shoulders are set, while I make out his fists, visibly clenched in his pocket. His deep brown eyes are piercing into mine and he actually looks dangerous, yet sexy as hell at the same time.

"Boyd, wait for me in the office while I fix us a drink." His head snaps to the side and that's when I see his pal from the other night. He nods in my direction and I offer him a small smile in return. Jensen doesn't say anything to me or Joey, as he helps himself to a beer. He doesn't so much as glance in my direction again, and I hate myself for it, but I can't help feeling a little bit disappointed.

"Someone's clearly pissed." Joey whistles beside me.

"No shit. Think yourself lucky that you don't have to live with him."

"You know my offers always there for you to share my bed, sugar."

"Enough." I plead with him, while he laughs at me. "Just fucking quit it, Joe."

"Excuse me."

"Hey, what can I get you?" I ask the small, petite brunette who is stood before me. "You want a special? This guy here does amazing cocktails, but don't let him know I told you that." Smiling, I signal to Joey, where he's resting up against the till.

"Um, no actually. I'm looking for Jensen. Is he here?"

"Who's asking?" I'm not sure what the code is if someone asks for the boss. Maybe he doesn't want people to know that he's here.

"Does that matter? If he's around, let him know that Minnie is here, and I'll have a wine soda while I wait."

"Joe, bring this lady a wine soda ASAP." It's about time that guy did something before he clocks off anyway. "I'll just go grab him for you now... *Minnie*." I try her name on my tongue and I'm not sure if I like it. I knock once on the office door, but there's no answer so I walk straight in. I instantly smell smoke as I enter and can't help but cough as I'm suddenly restricted of air from the fumes.

"What?" Jensen says as he looks straight at me. It looks like he's still pissed off for some reason, but hey, that isn't my problem.

"You wanna open a window or something in here? There's some chick asking for you at the bar."

"And it starts..." Boyd laughs, while Jensen is still taking me in.

"Did you get a name?"

"Um, yeah, Molly. No, actually I think she said her name was Minnie." I could have imagined it, but both Boyd and Jensen's faces go slack with shock at the mention of her name. "Do you want me to send her through or...?"

"Send her through." Is all he says before

turning away from me and he continues his conversation with Boyd. I'm not going to lie, I feel pretty angry that he brushed me off like that. I don't know why, it's not as if I expected a thank you or anything, but still, for some reason my stomach begins to churn.

"Hey, Minnie? If you head in that direction you'll see the office. Jensen's in there."

"Thank you so, so, much. I owe you big time for this." I nod and watch her, as she turns on her tiny heels and heads towards the office. Jensen looked pretty shocked to hear her name, as did Boyd, so her arrival mustn't have been planned. Oh well, like I've said before, it isn't my drama. I've got enough of that going on right now as it is.

"You want a lift back?" I look up from where I am crouched down restocking the fridge and see Jensen stood over me. He has a powerful stance. Even when he has his hip propped up against the counter, all relaxed, he still looks dangerous.

"I'm good, but thanks." I say, deciding that being polite in declining his offer is the best way to go. Why is he offering me a lift home? Minnie and Boyd are stood in the far corner of the bar. "Shouldn't you be over there?" I calmly say, as I point in the opposite direction.

"How are you going to get home? You're not walking on your own." He completely avoids my question, while still giving me orders. It's as if he doesn't realise he's doing it.

"In case it skipped your attention, I'm a fully grown woman and I can look after myself." I snap, unable to contain my frustration when it comes to him. He steps closer to me and I soon find myself backed up against the wall as I try to get some distance between us.

"If you're staying with me, then I have a duty to make sure you get home safely. If you want to be a bitch about it, then that's fine, stay here for all I care. Just don't come moaning to me if some douche tries to hit on you." He snarls. I watch him retreat back to his friends or whatever they are, without a backwards glance in my direction. Oh fuck. I'd completely forgotten that Joey had already left for the night, so it looks like I'll be getting a cab, again. I guess that's better than being in an enclosed space with Jensen.

I arrive home not long after two in the morning, and I can't wait to jump in bed. It's been an emotional and mentally exhausting day and I can't wait to see the back of it. I'd decided to stay late to clean the bar properly and clear my head, but all that did was make me overthink even more. Maybe I should really think about going back to California. Surely I can't be worse of there, than I am here in Boston? As long as I don't go home, I'm sure I'd be okay. All I need is confirmation that he isn't around there anymore, and I can go home. The question is, how would I begin to find that kind of information out, without raising any suspicions?

The house is dark as I approach the driveway, and I sit and debate silently to myself, as to whether or not I should go in. This is getting ridiculous. Of course I should go in. I've lived here longer than this guy and whether he owns the place or not, I'm not going to let him push me out. Not without a fight anyway.

"For fucks sake!" I shout as I once again go crashing into something hard in the hallway. "Why can't you move these fucking boxes out of the goddamn way." I shout to the darkness.

"Watch where you're going then. Have you never heard of switching on the lights?"

"I thought you were in bed." My hand shuffles along the wall, while trying find the switch. When I find it and flick it down, I come face to face with Jensen standing before me in just a loose pair of sweats. He's smiling right at me. It's a nice smile, he looks relaxed, carefree and happy and it suits him. "What's with you?"

"You didn't want to disturb me? That's sweet. I thought you'd be coming for me with a pitchfork."

"I was brought up with manners, so I use them."

"You do? Jeez. You could have fooled me with the way you've been acting this past week."

"I've got my reasons. Now, if you'll excuse me, I'm going to bed."

"Anna." He shouts after me as I reach the stairs. I turn to look back at him and he looks so fucking beautiful. "Have a drink with me?"

By body almost instantly draws towards the idea of being close to him, but my head's telling me to carry on up those stairs. *"He's nothing but bad news. You've only just escaped the mess you were in. Do you really want to go back there?"* My voice chimes in my head. "Thanks, but I think I'm gonna call it a night. It's been one hell of a day."

"No worries. I'll see you tomorrow then. Good night."

"Yeah, night." The journey up the stairs feels like the longest one that I've had to take, with each step knowing that I'm dragging myself further and further away from Jensen.

JENSEN

My fucking balls are going to explode and all that she seems to do is walk around in tight arse clothes to torment the fucking shit out of me. I've been sat in the kitchen since five this morning and it's almost eight o'clock. I can hear Anna moving around upstairs, so I get up and make her a coffee. Her smart arse mouth is starting to grow on me the more time that I spend with her and fucking hell, she's killing me every goddamn day. I'm obviously not her favourite person, and she isn't mine, but while we're living together we may as swell make the most of it.

"Um, hi. Do you even sleep?" She asks as soon as she steps into the small kitchen area.

"Sleeping's for losers." I reply and get an evil look for my comment and I can't help but laugh at her. "Coffee?"

"Yeah, please."

"You feeling okay? You would have normally bitten my head off by now?" Maybe she's coming down with something. She does look pretty flushed, or that could just be because I bring out that effect in her.

"Yeah, well thank your lucky stars that I'm exhausted. I'm struggling to sleep right now."

"You are, huh? Maybe I could help with that? What's the point in sharing this house if we don't put it to good use? I can guarantee that once I'm done with you, you'll happily sleep for a week."

I wait for a smart arse response to my comment, but nothing comes from those delectable lips. Instead, she sits down at the table and stares at me whilst trying to figure me out.

"What's your story Jensen?"

"I don't have much to tell. You on the other hand seem to be hiding something and I want to know what it is." She stays quiet for a while, mulling over what she does and doesn't want to say, so I allow her the time she needs. I'm not used to waiting, but something about her wants me to.

"I'm just a private person. Why did you move here?"

"I move around, a lot. I don't normally stay in the same place for too long. Shit gets boring and predictable, you know? So when I'm done, I up and leave. It just so happens that I was looking for a new place to move to, and then bam, I bumped into your cousin who offered me this place. Kind of made sense to take her up on the offer." *All the fucking better for bumping into you.* I think to myself.

"I still don't know why she's done that. It makes no sense, whatsoever. This place and the bar mean everything to her. I wish I could grab her and give her a bloody good shake."

"Maybe she wanted a new challenge, or who knows, she might have wanted to start over again. That guy she's with obviously means a lot to her. Sometimes you need to take chances, otherwise you'll end up living the rest of your life with nothing but a whole bunch of what if's. I don't know about you, but I sure as hell ain't gonna live my life like that."

"Sometimes it's a lot easier said than done." She says so quietly, that I barely hear her. I knew it. I knew that there was something eating at her somewhere. Now I just need to find out what it is. I shouldn't be bothered, but I am. If this is the root cause of her being a bitch, then maybe, just maybe, I can get to the bottom of it for her.

"What you doing today?" I ask as I walk back into the living area. Anna is sat at the table with her head down, while scribbling frantically on the paper lay out before her. "Fucking hell, is that all you ever do?"

"Excuse me?" She asks and her voice rises as she glares at me.

"Woah. Calm the fuck down. All I'm saying is you're either working, or you're working. What the hell do you do for fun?"

"I can have as much fun as I want once this course is finished. I've already fallen behind and I can't afford for it to happen again."

"Okay, fair enough. Well get your shoes on. We're going to eat." No way is she sitting in, working on that paper all day, without getting something in her stomach.

"I've just told you I'm busy."

"And I've just told you to get your fucking shoes on. You want to be a hermit, then that's your problem, but if I say I'm shouting you to lunch, then I'm shouting you to lunch. You hear me?" Fucking hell. Why is she so hard to work or talk with? I'm gonna crack this chick if it's the last thing that I fucking do.

"Has anyone ever told you that you're a demanding bastard."

"Every goddamn day baby, now get that fine arse of yours out of that goddamn door, before I carry you out."

We pull up outside the nearest diner that I could find. The drive was pretty quiet; Anna clearly has a stick still firmly stuck up her arse or some shit. It seems like we're making progress and then, bam, out of nowhere she's the fucking she devil again.

"Do you want me to go?" I ask, turning my

head to the left slightly, so that I can gage her reaction better. It's taking everything that I have not to lean in closer and kiss her, again. She's fucking addictive.

"What, as in town?" Her voice is void of any emotion. Her face is expressionless, as if she's hiding away from something huge, and doesn't want me to see how vulnerable she really is beneath that hard exterior that she wears so well.

"Listen, if I'm the only thing thats causing you to be miserable, then I'll move out until you find somewhere to go. You've obviously got your own shit going on that you need to deal with. I might be a *prick*, as you so kindly out it, but underneath as of this," I wave my hands up and around my body, "I'm quite a reasonable guy. I understand people have opinions and I'm all for that. Hate on me as much as you want; but if I'm making someone's life hell, unintentionally, then I'll remove myself from the picture. It's not my plan to make your life harder than it already seems to be." Anna remains silent for some time, and I decide to leave her with her thoughts, so that she can process what I said. "Well, this mother fucker is hungry, you comin' or what?"

Fuck she gets under my skin like nothing I've known before. Why am I even bothering with her? She's so far up her own fucking arse and obviously thinks she's better than everyone else. "*Well, I've got fucking news for you sunshine, all you are, is a hot piece of arse.*"

ANNA

"I don't mean to be a bitch." I say as I sit facing him across the table. His eyes look up to meet mine and in this moment, a look of vulnerability passes over his features. "I guess what I'm trying to say is, you rub me up the wrong fucking way. You speak to me like shit. One day, you just came waltzing into Temptation out of nowhere and took my bar from me, not to mention you think you have the right to boss me around while I'm there. So excuse me if I come across a little heated sometimes." That bar was all I had left to keep me sane while I'm here.

"But I do..." He starts, but I cut him off. I need to say what's been playing on my mind.

"No, you don't. You don't have any right to

boss me around, whatsoever. If that's what you want, then hire someone else who is prepared to take your demands. I work fucking hard Jensen. I always have and I always will, but the minute someone starts to take the piss, I'm outta there. Treat me right and I'll be loyal to you no end, but when I'm being taken for granted, or having the piss taken out of me, that's when things get ugly. I don't like bullshit Jensen. I've dealt with enough of it to last me a lifetime and I'm not prepared to go through it again. Not for anyone."

"What can I get you today?" I look up and see that a waitress has app reared and is standing at our table, ready to take our order. She's quite petite, with her auburn hair thrown back into a pony-tail and just a hint of make-up around her dark blue eyes. I watch the way her eyes linger over Jensen's tattoos and jealously suddenly burns me up inside. Wow. Why the hell am I getting jealous over a fucking waitress? *Get yourself together Anna.*

"Um, yeah, I'll have the eggs and bacon with a latte." My words come out on an unintentional snap in the waitress' direction and Jensen quickly looks at me. He must sense my mood and tone, as he offers me a mega-watt smile.

"And what can I get for you?" She asks Jensen, her eyelashes going ten to the dozen, as she practically acts like I don't exist. Who is this girl, and does she know how desperate she looks?

"You, on my car, in nothing but your

panties." He says to the waitress. I cannot believe he has actually just said that to her. He really has no fucking shame. I guess it's his dick though and I'm pretty sure he can stick it wherever he wants. It's his problem if he wants a glow stick.

"Um... I..." She says, suddenly lost for words and her cheeks are flushed with a hint of red, displaying her embarrassment. Obviously she didn't expect that kind response from him.

"I'll have what she's having." He laughs and throws in a cheeky grin especially for her. The waitress quickly scribbles down our order and scurries back towards the kitchen. Jensen looks at me, still feeling happy with himself. "What?"

"You're an animal Jensen Blake. Do you know that?" I scowl.

"You know it. Don't start getting jealous on me, Anna. I don't dig jealous chicks. Plus, I offered you a piece of this first," He makes sure to slowly trail his finger down that very defined torso before continuing, "and you turned me down. I'm a hot-blooded male after all, and this male has some pretty hot needs. What do you expect me to do, go bust one out in the bathroom?"

"Well go after her then. Just don't expect me to wait around while you get your cheap thrills." I snap. Normally I wouldn't give two hoots if someone who I was eating with, decided to check out the staff, maybe pick them up, usually I'd be all for it, but seeing Jensen do it pisses me right off. Maybe it's best if he does find somewhere else to stay until I sort myself out. Being around him isn't healthy for me and my recovering mind. I moved here to get away from the drama that guys like him create. This was supposed to be a fresh start for me, and look how well that's going.

"You gonna eat that?" He asks, pulling me out of my thoughts. I don't know how long I have been sitting here, just staring into my latte, while Jensen shoots glances across to the waitress. I'm not sure if he's doing it to piss me off, but deciding to ignore him doesn't seem to be doing me any favours.

"No. You want it?" I ask. Suddenly I don't want to be here anymore. Lunch with Jensen sounded like a perfect idea for us to get to know each other, see if maybe we could get on; but all it's proving is that we're explosive when we're together.

"You betcha." He replies as he leans over slightly and snatches my plate. I know he's a man, but the portions here aren't exactly small, and there's not so much as a crumb left on his plate. He notices me eyeing him suspiciously and gives me a wink. "What? I've worked up an appetite, what's the big deal?"

Okay, that's way too much information for me. He's clearly goading me here, but still, there's no need for him to be a twat about it. "There's some stuff I've gotta do before I head back home, so I'm off." I can't stand to be around him any longer. Hate combined with attraction doesn't mix well, or at least that's what I'm learning quickly the longer that I'm around him.

"Really? You didn't mention it earlier?" His eyebrows are raised and I know he doesn't believe it one bit.

"I wasn't aware that I had to tell you my plans?" I can see this conversation getting pretty heated, pretty quickly. I stand and grab my bag and as I turn to leave, Jensen calls the waitress over from earlier, purely so that I can hear, I'm not to sure why, but it pisses me off no-end. Who the fuck does he think he is?

I have no idea where I'm going to go to help pass the next few hours. Leaving without a form of transport wasn't one of my greatest ideas, but it's too late to turn back now. It's not like I'm comfortable with walking back into the diner just to interrupt Jensen and his little floozy's catch-up. Fuck. Why am I even letting this get to me? Who am I to care who he talks to? *"I don't even like the guy."* I think to myself, in the hope that, the more I repeat it, the more I'm likely to believe it myself. All this stuff with Holly is messing with my head and I need to put a stop to it as soon as possible, I just haven't got a clue where to start.

After what's got to be the longest bus journey known to man, I hop off just outside Temptation. I know I won't need to worry about Jensen arriving back anytime soon, as he looked like he'll be busy for some time, when I left him chatting up some floozy. What I need is a stiff drink, maybe two, to get rid of these confusing feelings that are running wild through my system.

"Yo, Anna. What are you doing here? You're not rota'd on today."

"I know, I know. Believe it or not Joe, I'm actually here for pleasure. Make me a double vodka soda, with lime and hold the ice. Oh, and some of those shots, the ones that we had last time." I say, as I pull myself up on the barstool. Joe looks at me like I've lost the plot, but I couldn't give two hoots.

"Oh...Kay." He whistles but asks no questions and gets straight to work, which I'm grateful for.

"Who's the chick?" I point to the far side of the bar where a tall, brunette stands, flicking her glossy hair as she wipes the bar down. Joey follows my line of sight and smiles.

"That right there is Darcie. She's a temp apparently. She started today. Girl, have you seen that arse? My working hours just got fun and my time off even hotter." Un-fucking-real. Joey's like a horny fucking teenager. What am I missing here? They're all at it like it's going out of fashion.

"Joe, you can't keep scaring the bar staff away. It's bad enough with the punters already." I laugh, suddenly feeling much more comfortable in my familiar surroundings. Temptation has definitely brought me some good times and heaps of distractions to get me through the dark times. To be honest, I'd probably crumble if I didn't get to work here anymore. It's not even worth thinking about.

"Oh yeah, you laugh all you want. I've got a feeling that this one's going to be different. Trust me Anna, it's time to get me some real action."

"Isn't that what you've been getting every night, anyway?"

"See, that's what I thought I was getting, right up until this little beauty came walking into my life. Anna, I could practically see her wings shine, as she walked through those doors. Everything around me just stopped, as if she'd frozen time, just to make sure that I noticed her."

"Goddamnit, Joe. Do me a favour, and fucking shoot me now!" There is no way that I'm going to take him seriously. I wouldn't even be able to count the amount of chicks that he's hit on, swore they were the one, just for him to have it thrown back in his face within five minutes, over the past week. "Joey; a word of advice. Tread carefully with this one. She looks like she'd eat you alive."

"Oh, you have no idea how much I'm hoping for that to happen."

"Stick another one of those in there will you?" I ask, as I neck the rest of my drink and slide it towards him on the opposite side of the bar and then chase it up with the shots. Fuck, my throat burns, but the intensity of the shot is a welcome distraction from my racing mind, even if it is for a few seconds.

"Anna, it's just gone three in the afternoon and you don't even drink. What the hell's going on? You wanna talk about it?"

"Am I paying customer?" I ask, as I raise my eyebrows at him? "Well?"

"Yeah, but..."

"Just stick the fucking drink in the glass Joe. Please, I don't need shit from you too."

"Okay, okay. I'm just sayin' that I'm here if you need me, you know to talk, or some shit?"

"Hey there. Is he bothering you Miss?" Tilting my head to the side I see Darcie, or whatever she is called, approaching me. "Joe, maybe you should leave her alone. She might just want to have a quiet drink." Her smile is perfect, and highly attractive and I suddenly find myself feeling a little self-conscious around her.

"It's okay." I smile, unsure what else to say. Is she actually making her mark on him already? Bloody looks like it to me.

"Darcie, this is Anna. She runs, I mean did run..." Joey stumbles.

"I work here, is what he's trying to say."

"Does Jensen know that you're here drinking? He won't be happy if you're drinking on the job." Her attitude changes, instantly. Gone is her flawless smile, and a fierce scowl is plastered on her face.

"So today's your first day, am I right?" I ask. "Well how about I let you in on a little secret. Jensen doesn't tell me shit." The words fly out of my mouth, the alcohol in my system removing any filter that I would normally have. Darcie looks taken aback and gives Joey a worried glance.

"Anna, Darcie didn't mean..."

"I don't really care what she meant Joey, I've come here for a drink, you know, to clear my head of the bullshit, just to try and forget everything that's pilling up on top of me, not to be bombarded with questions and people chiming in with their unwanted fucking opinions." After my outburst, Joey leaves me be and I actually don't see him for a while and I try to relax.

As the hours pass by, the bar begins to get crowded and I take that as my cue to leave. Once again, I'm without a coat and the weather is getting colder and colder with each day that passes. In my defence, I hadn't set out on coming here when I left the house earlier, so what's a girl to do?

The house is quiet as I walk through the hallway and I'm glad as Jensen doesn't seem to be back yet. I don't think I could face him, not now, not while I'm in this state. I don't drink often. I've witnessed too many people turn from it. Being sober and witnessing what those people turn into is bad enough, but today I just needed something to numb the anxiety, the fear; the unwanted feelings around Jensen. Just something to make it stop and I know I'll be paying for it tomorrow.

"Enjoy yourself?"

I look over to the kitchen table and see Jensen seated there, positioned in his new found favourite place at the kitchen table, wearing an unmistakable face of thunder as he looks at me.

"Excuse me?" I say, unsure what he's getting at, or why it has anything to do with him.

"I thought you had stuff that you needed to do?" Leaning forward on the chair, his eyes pierce into me and I suddenly feel like I should be apologising for something. *"Anna, you have nothing to apologise for here. You went for a drink, surrounded by colleagues. There's nothing wrong with that."* I mentally tell myself.

"Yeah, I did. What's with the questions?" I stumble a little, as I try to grab some water from the kitchen tap, and almost fall flat on my arse. I just about grab the side unit in time, before things get embarrassing.

"What like getting pissed at Temptation?" I can tell without looking at him that he's pissed, but he has no right to be. He really needs to come down from his power trip and fast.

"What, am I not allowed to drink now? Why are you checking up on me anyway? It's got nothing to do with you what I do in my spare time." I say as I turn to look at him.

"I got a call from Joey. He was pretty worried about you and I was this close," he pinches his thumb and forefinger together to emphasise his point, "to getting in my car and coming after you."

"You've got to be kidding me?" I can't help but laugh. Are these guys for real? I go out and let my hair down for a little while and they all come out in force. Is my life that fucking bad, that all hell breaks loose if I have a drink?

"Listen Anna, I know what guys can do. Shit, I've fucking seen them prey on girls like you and it isn't fucking pretty. So, my bad, for fucking caring and worrying if anything had happened to you."

"Oh yeah, and I don't know? You know shit about me, so butt the fuck out of my business." Within seconds he's by my side and I go numb, from the proximity of him or the alcohol, I can't be sure.

"I'm making it my fucking business." His lips come crashing down against mine, rough and needy at the same time. They move with such a forceful passion, desperately seeking for a response or reaction from mine. Against every bone in my body, my mouth co-operates willingly with his and my body goes lax, as I find myself pressed against him. His big strong arms slowly trail up my side and his hands, and once they have reached their destination, tenderly cup each side of my face. I shouldn't be doing this, somewhere in the back of my fucked up head, I know that I will regret this in the morning; but right now, I need to find my own release and escape for just a little while.

"Jensen…" I moan against him, revelling in this feeling of contentment that I'm now in. Slowly, I trail my fingers down his torso and I memorise every hard, defined muscle in my mind. He shudders a little under my touch, a moan escaping from deep within him, while never taking his lips away from mine. Knowing that he wants this just as much as me; gives me the strength that I need to continue exploring his manly body. I find my arms being placed above my head as Jensen slowly pulls my top up, and away from my body, so that my bare skin is exposed to him.

"Damn, Anna." His eyes flicker back to mine once he's taken me in, and the heat within them sends a raging fire through my veins, setting off multiple explosions all over my body. How can someone be so turned on from one look alone? *"If he's this good at undressing me, he must be fucking Dynamite in bed."* I say to myself, while breathing rapidly, trying with everything that I have to calm myself down. My fingers instantly fall on to his sleeve of tattoos, and I trace the lines gently. So many memories, so many stories could be in this tattoo and I can't help but wonder what his life was like before he arrived here in Boston.

"I like this. I like how mysterious it looks." I whisper, without looking at him, my eyes transfixed on the intricate designs. There is so much detail, that every time I look over it, I see something new.

"If only you knew what was behind it, but I'm sure you'll agree that sometimes things are better left unsaid." I don't have time to ask him what he means, as he scoops me up into his arms, with both of my legs wrapped tightly around his waist as he walks us both to the stairs. "You sure you want to do this? This is your last chance to back out." He asks me, and all I can do is nod, before my lips find his once again. I don't want to think anymore, I'm fed up of thinking all the time. It never stops, even when I sleep, and it's mentally draining. I want, no; I need something to help me forget and this, with Jensen, seems like the perfect cure, *for now*.

As we enter my bedroom, he lowers me down slowly, so that every part of my body feels every part of his, as he holds me tight against him. His lips find the curve of my neck, teasing me slowly, as he kisses as licks his way down my body, stopping at each curve of my breasts, until continuing his assault on me with his mouth, working his way gently down to my stomach. I have no words. Nothing but Jensen and what he is doing to me is running through my mind. With the alcohol still flowing in my system, I'm not as self-conscious as I normally would be, and I feel a hell of a lot more bolder than usual. I run my fingers through his hair, while he slowly begins to unbutton my jeans. I catch sight of my reflection in the mirror and Jensen follows my line of sight. A wicked smile spreads across his face and I can't help finding the danger that glistens in his eyes, sexy as hell.

"Follow me." He demands, and I'm in no fit state to deny him anything at this point. My skin suddenly feels bare and cold without his touch, causing me to shiver and I need to have him close to me again. He walks over to the floor length mirror and positions me right in front of it, so all that I can see is my flushed, heated, half-naked body in the reflection. Jensen is positioned behind me and his eyes blaze with heated desire.

"I want you to see exactly what I see, Anna. Don't close those Bambi eyes." He whispers against my ear, causing an ice-cold shiver and goosebumps ripple over my skin. All of my senses are on high alert and all I want, is for him to touch me, not look at me. "I want you to watch what my touch does to your body. I want you to see how your body reacts when you come undone as I pleasure your every need."

"Mmm." I moan as his hand trails slowly up my side again, only this time I'm looking at his eyes through the mirror. This way feels more sensual somehow, and knowing that I can see everything that he is doing, is driving me crazy inside. My breasts feel heavy as Jensen frees them from within my bra, but he doesn't go to them straight away. Instead, he slowly removes my pants and bends down behind me. I have no clue what he's doing as the only light in my bedroom comes from the hallway, casting a dim glow.

"I want you to touch yourself Anna. Slowly touch yourself where you want me to touch you." Without thinking, my hands automatically cup my breasts, as I ache for him to touch me there. All my inhibitions have gone out of the window as I work my hands around my body, closing my eyes and imaging that it was Jensen's hands on me.

"Keep your eyes open." He snaps, and my eyes fly open. I'm aroused beyond anything that I have ever known, and all he is doing, is torturing me here, and he sure as hell knows it too. His hands snake up my legs, and I place my feet further apart to give him the access that he needs, but he completely skips that area of my body. At any moment, I could combust, but he's delaying it for as long as possible and it's driving me insane. Instead, he stands and lifts me up, before walking over to the bed. "You're so fucking hot Anna Jameson and you've done nothing but drive me fucking crazy since I met you."

I lie back on the bed, propped up slightly on my shoulders as I watch this beautiful, yet dangerous man before me. He never breaks eye contact with me as he places my panties between his teeth and pulls them slowly down my body, bit by bit. As I lay here, I'm amazed at the care and attention that he is paying to my body. I presumed he would be the type of guy that didn't mess around and was out for a quick fuck. Well, that's what I was hoping this would be. A quickie to block out the past, but the more time I spend with him like this, the more I appreciate him taking the time to worship my body. As soon as he is nestled in between my legs, I can't stop myself from pushing my hips up, hoping he'll take the fucking hint.

"Is there something that you need?" He asks, a knowing smirk, creeping onto his playful face.

"Don't make me wait anymore, Jensen. I can't take much more of this, it's killing me." I plead and I'm not ashamed. I'll fucking beg if I have too. The bed dips, as his weight is pressed down on top of me, both of his elbows resting on either side of my head. I feel the tip of him press against me, and he gently lowers himself into me, taking his sweet fucking time. Bollocks to this, I'm not made of glass and we're not exactly making sweet, sweet love. As soon as his lips connect with mine, I grip his arse and push him into me, hard. I let out a deep, satisfied moan, as he finally fills me and it feels fucking amazing. It's been so long since I've had any kind of release and it's only now, as he moves so perfectly in and out of me, that I realise just how much I need this. How much I need him.

I wake up and my head feels cloudy, my mouth drier than I've ever known it before, and I feel sick. Slowly, images from yesterday begin to filter thought my mind. Lunch with Jensen, then that floozy of a waitress making my day go from bad to worse. Then my brilliant idea of the day, deciding to rock up to Temptation to drink my problems away, only to come home to a disapproving Jensen. Oh fuck! No, no, no. I quickly pull the quilts back and see that I'm naked. Oh my god. How could I be so fucking stupid. Why did I sleep with Jensen of all people? I slowly turn over and see that my bed is empty. Dread and shame fill me as I run my hands down my face. Don't get me wrong, last night was amazing, perfect even. But now I have to face him while I'm sober. I don't want to be one of those girls who can be classed as a victorious accomplishment. Shit, shit, shit, why couldn't I just say no? *"Because you wanted it too, and you were enjoying it too much too stop."* I contemplate on hiding away in my room for as long as I can, until I suddenly realise that I need to get to class. Maybe I could call in and say I'm not well? All of a sudden, I sure as hell don't feel it. A hot shower is what I need to try and wash Jensen away from my body. Maybe then, I'll be able to create a plan of action as to what I'm going to say to him. How am I even going to be able to look him in the eye, after everything that we did last night? He did things to me, that I never even knew existed.

"How do?" I spin on my heels at the sound of that deep rustic voice. I should know by now, that when the house is quiet, he's most likely brooding in a corner somewhere. As usual, he's sat in his favourite spot at the table. Please don't tell me he wants to make small talk. Who knows, maybe he regrets what happened last night and he won't even bother bringing it up.

"Hey." I say sheepishly, deciding my glass of water can wait. "I didn't know you were home."

"I can leave a daily diary entry on the fridge each morning if you like?" He laughs at me. I suddenly feel exposed and vulnerable around him, and I can feel the panic begin to set in.

"No, I'm good, I don't think I need to know what you get up to when you're not around. Anyway, I'm in a rush so I'll see you later." I mentally slap myself for my comment. No, I don't want to see him later; it's bad enough that I've just had to see him now. I need to get my head around what happened last night, before I do anything with Jensen. As he sits there with his ruffled hair in only his sweat pants, images and feelings of last night overcome me and my face heats from the memory of that delicious mouth of his. If I can feel the heat of my face right now, he sure as hell can see it.

"You want a ride? I'm heading out now anyways?" He asks while his cocky smirk dances along his rugged features. Is he taking the piss?

"Erm… no, I'm okay, really, but thanks." This is so awkward. All he does is give me a quick shrug of his shoulders as he leaves the kitchen. I don't know if I was secretly hoping for him to bring up last night, maybe make a sly comment about it, but he says nothing, as if nothing actually happened. I suddenly feel used and cheap, but I guess I've only got myself to blame, and this is what I was worried about when I woke up this morning.

ANNA

As I walk into Temptation for the start of my shift, I notice Darcie propped up against the bar and I get a sudden, unwelcome flashback from last night. Visions of me being an absolute bitch, just because I was pissed off, flash across my mind's eye. I make my way towards her, unsure of what I'm going to say, but I know that I need to apologise for my outburst last night. There was no need whatsoever for the way that I spoke to her and I feel so bad. Just as I put my foot forward to approach her, I hear her soft laugh dance through the bar and then, out of nowhere, Jensen appears behind her and throws his arms around her waist. I stand motionless as he kisses the side of her neck, like he did with me last night and her giggling only intensifies. Stood at a distance, with the bar lights shining down on them, I can see both of them smiling brightly, wearing what can only be described as *I've just been royally fucked good and proper* expressions. Jensen's hair is all over the place, like hands have recently been entwining and pulling on it. Nausea courses through me, knowing that it was my bed he was in last night and my body that he was pleasuring, and now he's quickly moved on to his latest victim. Fucking hell, is this guy just employing chicks to shag? Deciding that I'm going to be the bigger person here, and not let Jensen see how much this is effecting me, I walk straight to the bar, my heels clicking along the floor as I go, acting as if I haven't got a care in the world. I sense both of them looking at me as I approach but I don't care that I've interrupted their fun. All I care about is getting some alcohol down me and fast.

"You're early, you don't start until eight." Jensen says as I reach for the vodka and pour myself a double shot.

"Yeah, I know." I respond before downing my drink. "I've got shit to do and it won't get done by itself will it?" I'm proud that I can walk away from them both with my head held high, showing no signs of how pissed off I really am. I wanted nothing more than to wipe that fake smile from Darcie's lips.

"*I have shit to do?*" That's probably the lamest excuse that I've come up with in a while. After thinking about nothing but last night, I thought it was best that, maybe, I should speak to Jensen about it. If not, us living together and avoiding the conversation is going to cause nothing but unwanted problems, and I don't think I can take any more of those right now. As soon as I got home and realised he wasn't there, I decided to come here, as this is the only other place I thought that he might be. Now I feel like such a fool, because last night was obviously just your standard night for Jensen. He's obviously got a way of making girls like me feel special, as if we're the only one for him, and then bam, you're dropped like you never fucking existed. Like he's said before; he's got needs and by that, he clearly means a different woman every night. No wonder he moves around so much, once all the woman have been used he tries a different county. Maybe this could be a blessing and I've had a lucky escape. That doesn't change the fact that I have to live and work with him.

While I'm here, I decide to pass the hours by doing some work for my upcoming assignment, but nothing seems to be happening. I've managed two lines on my assignment so far and I just can't make my mind focus, at all. Maybe a familiar voice will soothe me of my problems. I bloody hope so anyway and I won't know unless I try. Picking up my phone, I weigh up in mind if I should call, or keep my distance, like I promised myself that I would. I need to remember that I can't do this all the time. It's got to be a one off.

"Hey, it's me." I say with a faint smile when I hear his voice on the other end of the line.

"Anna, it's good to hear from you."

"So, how have you been?" I fiddle with the papers in front of me, as my nerves kick in.

"Good. Same old, you know? What about you?"

"Yeah, I'm okay. I could be better, but that's life I guess. I'm sorry about the other day; it was a shock hearing from you."

"Anna, don't you dare apologise. I get it and it's fine. You sure you're okay? You don't sound too good."

"No dad, I'm not. I don't think I can do this anymore. Everything's just going from bad to worse and I don't know how to stop any of it. It's getting out of control"

"Come home, then. As soon as you're back in your comfort zone, maybe you'll feel a bit better?"

"I wish it was that simple dad, really I do, but I can't. At least not yet anyway." I would go back home to my dad and the life that I had before in a heartbeat, but that's wishful thinking on a completely different scale and the sooner I admit that to myself, the better I'll be at trying to move past this.

"But why?" I hear his temper flare by the tone of his voice. I know I'm hurting him and he's frustrated with my cryptic explanations, jeez, he has every right to be, but it has to be this way.

"Dad, honestly if it was that easy, believe

me; I'd be home in a heartbeat."

"Honey, I'm sure that whatever it is, we can get through it. How about I come to you?" Now that sounds like a great idea, but I'd be too scared that he'll be followed, or something bad will happen to him because of me. I've done a pretty good job of keeping him safe and completely out of this mess so far, and I plan to keep it that way.

"I'll be back soon, I'm sure. I just can't say when, Dad. I've got Holly's crap to deal with here and I can't leave it in this mess." I tell him. Okay, so it's not the whole truth but it's not a complete lie either. "I miss you, Dad."

"I miss you too honey, don't you ever forget that. You call me if you need anything, day or night; you hear me?"

"Yeah." A stray tear falls down my cheek. I don't deserve my dad's kindness, especially after the way I treated him and everything that I put him through. I really did expect him to disown me. The fact that he still wants to keep in touch with me, causes my heart to swell in my chest.

"Okay, well I'll let you get back to *Holly's crap* as you so nicely put it, but make sure you call me soon, okay?"

"I will, Dad, I promise. I love you."

"I love you too, honey."

Tonight of all nights, the bar is practically dead. I love being busy, it keeps my mind active and focused, instead of wandering off to other things that I wish I could forget. Yet, now as I stand here waiting to serve someone, all that's going through my mind is knowing that Jensen has disappeared with our new barmaid. Jealousy consumes me and I hate myself for it. That guy really has no shame. I guess he really will stick his dick anywhere purely for his pleasure. Life at home sure is going to get interesting now. One thing I swore to myself when I left California, was that I would never be used again. I switched everything off so that I could start again. I walked away from everyone I knew, everyone that I grew up with, just so that I could try and make amends for the horrible trap that I had fallen into. Deep down, I think that's why I took a dislike to Jensen to begin with, because I knew something like this would happen, and low and behold, it has. I'd love to blame Holly for this too, but she didn't force me to jump into bed with him just so I could try a new kind of distraction. No, I did that all by my little old self.

"Earth to Anna." Joey waves his hands frantically in front of my face to get my attention. I barely recognise him at first.

"Hey, you. Hang on, it's Wednesday night. Why are you here?" Surprisingly, he looks fresh faced and his eyes sparkle instead of looking glazed from alcohol and all that other crap that he takes to have what *he* calls a *good time.* He's actually looking pretty good, I have to admit. "You scrub up pretty well, Joe."

"I've got myself a hot date, haven't I?" The smug look on his face has me smiling instantly. He looks so pleased for himself and this makes me happy.

"Oh yeah? Who's the lucky chick that's getting some hot Joey action tonight?" I ask, unsure if I want to know the answer. It could be anyone of these poor souls.

"She's hot dude, and by hot, I mean smoking. You remember Darcie from last night, right? The one who's ears you chewed off?"

"Really?" I'm a little shocked to say the least. Joey must have read the signs completely wrong. "Are you sure, you asked her and didn't assume it was a date?"

"Of course I'm sure. It's gonna be one heck of a ride too. I'll have a pint while I wait, if you don't mind, Miss."

Oh, poor Joe. I can tell he's got the hot's for this chick real bad and I don't want to be the one to burst his bubble and tell him that she's currently hooked up with our man slag of a boss. Plus, saying it out loud will only validate that point, and I'm not ready to be a complete laughing stock just yet.

"You okay now? You didn't seem yourself yesterday."

"Yeah, about yesterday. Look I'm sorry. I was having a bad day and you were just in the wrong place at the wrong time. I didn't mean to be a bitch, Joe."

"Yeah you did. I may not have known you long, but I can tell when you're lying to me. Your nose wrinkles up in disgust, like you can smell your own bullshit."

"Is that right?" I slide his beer over to him,

still undecided if I should tell him where Darcie is. "Maybe next time you might want to hold back from calling Jensen to give him updates on my whereabouts, as if I'm his bitch."

"Anna, I was worried about you, is that so bad? You were doing shots like they were going out of fashion, and you hardly drink. I knew if I questioned you anymore then you'd flip your shit, so I called Jensen. He seemed like the best person to call seeing as though he lives with you. I asked him to keep an eye on you when you got home as you seemed to be in a bad place, that's all."

"I get that, just don't do it again, okay? I decided to let my hair down, you know, like you keep telling me? So what time's Darcie supposed to be here?"

"Not 'til around ten. Plus, you look like you could do with some company. Has it been this dead all night?"

"Yep, and it's been dragging like fucking crazy too."

I really want to tell Joey about Darcie before he gets his hopes up and ends up getting way ahead of himself. Would I prefer to potentially destroy some of his manliness now, or later when it's too late and he finds out that I knew about her slutty ways further on down the line. "Hey, Joe. About Darcie..."

"What about me?" I look over to see Darcie walking up to us in noting but a skimpy dress that, doesn't really leave much to the imagination. Her heavy chest is almost falling out of her top just from her walk, alone.

"Anna was just asking what time you'd be arriving."

"She was, huh?" Darcie looks over at me, as if daring me to say something about her and Jensen earlier. I'd love to but, I won't, and I'd really love to wipe that smug fucking look off of her face.

"Anna, how are we feeling today?" She says as she drapes one arm around Joe's shoulders, but her large green eyes still never leave mine.

"Oh I'm good, thanks. I came in earlier to apologise for last night, but you looked pretty occupied.I didn't want to interrupt." I smile ever so politely at her. Everything about her screams bitch, but I won't be making a show of myself for her benefit anytime soon, especially since she'll probably go running her mouth off to her new fuck buddy.

"You didn't tell me you saw Darcie earlier, Anna?"

"Didn't I? It must have slipped my mind. Like I said, you were pretty occupied weren't you?"

"Yeah, just learning the ropes again, you know?" Is that what you call it these days? It doesn't skip my attention that she said *again.* I'm not sure what to make of that comment just yet, but I can imagine it means that she's used to spreading her legs for the boss, or she's known Jensen for some time. Both thoughts cause me to shudder. "You miss me, handsome?" She plants a kiss on Joey's cheek and leaves a smear of blood red lipstick in its wake.

"Is Jensen coming in tonight?" I ask before I can stop myself. Why am I asking about Jensen, and why am I asking *her* of all people? Darcie looks up at me and smiles, displaying a perfect set of shiny whites.

"I'm not sure honey. I doubt it, when I last saw him, he looked pretty beat and was going home for a shower. You want me to call him, let him know that you were asking about him?"

"No, I'm sure it can wait, I'll see him when I get home anyway."

"Of course. I forget that you two live together. Can't be easy having to deal with him and his crazy shit on a daily basis, huh?"

"I wouldn't know. I'm hardly there most of the time." Why have I just told her this? Now she's probably going to turn up at my place at all hours and I'll be forced to hear those two go at it, while I'm all lonely, sat up in my room.

"Right handsome, where are you taking me on this hot date of ours?" Darcie looks back at me and winks. "Maybe I'll be seeing you at home, as well as work." Shitting hell, Anna. Always one to drop yourself in it.

The lights are on as I walk up the driveway, so I know that Jensen is definitely home. I try to avoid seeing him, but as I walk through the front door, Jensen is coming down the stairs in just his sweats. How I love to secretly watch him parading around the house half naked. The sight of him causes me to stop in my tracks and he just looks at me. There is no trace of emotion on his face, just a blank look that you might give to a stranger who you were weighing up, before deciding if you liked them or not.

"Hurry up, will you? You've been up there for ages. What's taking you so long?" A female voice calls through from the front room and I can't help but shake my head in disgust at him. Three, fucking women, in less than twenty-four hours. I need a shower to wash the feel of him against me that still seems to linger. Even though I scrubbed and scrubbed in the shower this morning, I can still feel him against my skin, I can smell him as if he is still firmly pressed against me, and all it does is remind me how stupid I have been. I don't say anything to him, instead, I walk straight past him on the stairs. He doesn't say anything to me either. As I continue my assent, he walks into the front room without looking back, no doubt into the arms of his next lay.

Once I'm showered and in my pyjamas, I curl up under my quilts and stick my headphones in and turn the volume right up. Having to see Jensen slag it about with other women is one thing, but no way will I sit back, and listen to him make another woman scream, the way he did with me.

JENSEN

The look on Anna's face as she walked through the door was fucking priceless. She might not want to talk about last night, or acknowledge that it happened, but there is something between us; I can feel it. Especially when she hears Minnie's voice filter from the living area, shit if looks could kill. I don't know what she wants from me. There's not a fucking chance, that I'm going to bring up last night. It's up to her to do that. I thought this morning would have turned out completely different. After she fell asleep lying in my arms, I really thought that we had made a breakthrough. I guess that's wishful-fucking-thinking on my part.

I can only imagine what she must think of

me. Walking into Temptation and seeing me with Darcie, to then come home and hear Minnie's voice filtering through from the front room as I make my way down the stairs in just my sweats. Yeah, me and Darcie go way back. We've had an agreement for years where we are there for each other when needed, but with none of those fucking complicated strings attached. We need a distraction, then, we distract each other for a little while. Heaps of fun, with no expectations. That's what life has always been about for me. At least it was, until the biggest complication that I have ever known landed right in front of my balls. *Anna fucking Jameson.*

Minnie on the other hand is something else entirely. No way on god's green earth would I sleep with her, ever. My fucking balls are worth more to me than some quick lay. Sure she's hot, but she belongs to someone else. She always has and she always will. We're good friends and she's always had my back no matter what. Throughout my entire life, Minnie has been there for me, and she's never once judged me for the decisions that I chose to make, and for that I'll always be grateful to her.

"What are you doing?" She chimes as I walk back through the door.

"Fucking hell, Min. Can a guy not use the loo in peace? Jeez."

"Oh right, my bad. I need to see him J. It's killing me just sitting around, unable to do anything to help, day in, day out, you know?" Unshed tears begin to sparkle in her eyes as she tries to hold back her emotions. Minnie has never liked to show her soft side, but sometimes you've got to let it out; otherwise, before you know it, you'll get swallowed up into that big black fucking hole and you won't be able to get back out as easily. Trust me, I fucking know. "Can you speak to him for me?"

"Sure, but I'm not sure if he'll get back to me. I waited months to hear from him last time. You know what he's like Min. He only makes contact if he needs to. He likes to play his cards close to his chest, and keep his family out of it."

"I need to know when he's coming home J. I don't know how much longer I can wait around for. I'm getting nothing from him, nada. And he expects me to just sit around and wait. The last time I tried to call and speak to him, he had my contact wiped. What kind of guy does that?"

"There's probably a reason why he hasn't been in touch and you know it. Mitchell doesn't do shit lightly. It'll be fucking killing him not speaking to you, trust me. I know how deep you two go, but I'll see what I can find out for you. Plus, he probably hates the fact that you know he's in there and he can't be here with you." I say. I don't know what else to say to her. I'm not going to start telling her what she wants to hear, that's never been my style. However, if I thought something would intentionally hurt her, then I might bend the truth a little bit, just to soften the blow. To be honest, I don't think Mitchell even knows that she's turned up here and I sure as hell don't want to tell her that he might be coming home soon, just for it all to go to shit. If she has to wait another five or so years to see Mitchell, I think it might actually kill her on the inside. Instead, all I can do is fill up her glass with some soothing amber liquid and give her shoulder a caring, brotherly squeeze.

The night passes by in a haze, Minnie seated quietly on the sofa and me mulling over the past twenty-four hours and its events. How did it get to this? Sure, Anna's hot as hell; there's no fucking denying it, but now that I've had a piece of her, I need so much fucking more. I can't get her out of my fucking mind and this morning when she straight up blanked what happened, I was pissed as hell. One night definitely isn't going to cut it with her. Never, have I ever had a woman do that to me before. Fuck, I was confused and I could tell she didn't want to talk about it. I was hoping if I could drive her to where she needed to be, then we could talk, but she blew me off then too. When I got to the bar, Darcie was already there, waiting for me to open up and it felt like I'd gone back a few years to when I opened up the doors to my first bar. The days when Darcie and I thought we could rule the fucking world. So I thought, what better way to forget my humiliation, than a distraction? Darcie has always been perfect whenever it came to me needing a distraction.

I have no fucking idea what time I passed

out, but I'm jolted awake by a bang. I prise my heavy eyes open to try and see where the noise is coming from but I can't see shit. Minnie is curled up beside me on the sofa, finally looking peaceful, instead of her frantic self that she has been the past few days. At least she's finally getting some sleep.

Bang... Bang...

I pull myself up from the sofa and see Anna in the kitchen slamming cupboard doors as she goes by, most likely making her morning coffee.

"What the fuck are you doing?" I shout, unsure why she's making so much noise. It's still dark outside so it's still got to be fucking early.

"What am I doing? I'm searching for the coffee, what does it look like I'm doing?" Oh, she's definitely got that stick back and it's stuck firmly up her arse.

"Well do it fucking quietly then, shit I'm trying to sleep."

"Yeah, I can see that." She says, her perfect eyebrows arched slightly. I'm confused for a minute and then follow her eyes to where she is looking behind me. *Minnie.* That explains the banging then. "Sorry if I *disturbed* you, maybe you should take that shit to your room. Not everyone wants to see it." The sarcasm in her tone is evident as hell. I want to tell her that it isn't what it looks like, but why should I? She's clearly made her mind up about me, and I haven't got shit to prove to her. She lives here, that's all. Shit, she shouldn't even be banging around like she owns the goddamn place, because she doesn't, not anymore. This house is mine and she's going to have to get used to that pretty god damn fast. If she doesn't like it, then she sure as hell knows where the door is.

"You finished with that racket, or you gonna keep going until the cupboards fall off?" I'm starting to get royally pissed with her attitude. She's uncontrollable, and crazy.

"My bad, I'm sorry,I wouldn't want to disturb your sleeping beauty. I guess that's pretty rude of me, right? Can I just say one thing? Clearly you and Darcie sleep with anything, I don't get it personally, but maybe you might want to get that checked." Her hand points down to my crotch.

"It's got fuck all to do with you, who I sleep with. What, because I gave you a good seeing to the other night, you think you can throw your demands around? Wake the fuck up Anna." Her face changes instantly as the spiteful words leave my lips. I know I've hurt her, shit I feel bad for hurting her, but what am I supposed to do? She goes hot to fucking cold all the time. So I've slept with her, I've now got to wait forever to sleep with her again and in the meantime wait around like a little virgin? I don't fucking think so. "Anna..."

"Sleeping with you was the worst mistake of my life, and believe me, that's saying something." She shouts at me and then storms out of the kitchen, towards the front door. I can't be sure and it could have been the light, but I think I saw tears in her eyes.

"Well, that went well. Wanna tell me what's been happening since I saw you last?" Minnie sits up on the sofa, amusement dancing over her not so innocent face.

"Leave it Min, it's not worth the ball ache of going over it all again."

"No? It doesn't look that way to me. I'd say she's got you firmly by the balls and you're too damn scared to admit it, J."

"What would you know?" I spit at her, not caring who I hurt anymore. My head is all over the place with Anna, that I'm losing the goddamn will to fucking live. Why does everything with women have to be so fucking dramatic?

"What would I know?" Her voice goes all squeaky and this can only mean that she's about to give me a lecture. "You seem to forget that I've known you a hell of a long time Jensen Blake. You were barely out of nappies when I met you. I know when something has effected you, and I sure as hell haven't seen you act this way before, so that tells me, this girl- you really like her."

"That's the thing Min, I don't know if I do. She drives me fucking crazy and her attitude stinks, yet something about her draws me in and it's making me go insane. I can't go about doing my day to day business without her running around constantly in my mind. Is she okay? How's she getting to work? What's her past that she pretends she isn't running from. It's fucking crazy."

"Yeah, I'd say you've got it pretty bad, dude. Do you dislike her attitude towards you, personally or in general? Maybe it's because she's drawn to you too, but she's too afraid to admit it, herself. Have you looked at it that way? You know, Mitchell and I were exactly the same. I hated him at first sight, couldn't stand him, but deep down I knew it was because I was attracted to him. I didn't want to care about him, but something inside just wouldn't give up and I took it out on him like crazy. We'd argue day and night trying to hide our true feelings for one another, but it was no good. In the end we eventually gave in and, well, you know the rest. Maybe living together is only intensifying everything for her. You know, making it harder for her to handle."

"C'mon, jeez, I don't do all this chick talk. I'm a bloke, I have a dick, and balls. We don't get mushy. If she wants to be a bitch, then that's her problem not mine. If she can't handle her emotions, then that's got nothing to do with me either." Fuck that, if I'm chasing after some girl. I never have and I never will. Plus there's plenty of other chicks out there just waiting to be found, so why should I settle for one?

"Whatever you say, J. The path hasn't exactly been plain-sailing for me and Mitchell either. We've had our battles, probably more than most and I know we're not in a great place right now, but when push comes to shove, I know that he'd fight for me every goddamn time, and you know why? Because, he cares. Yes, he's a bloke, with a dick and a set of balls, but when it comes to someone you love, or care about, that my friend is when you become a man."

"Wow. You still pissed from last night, or something? Since when have you been all fucking mushy?" What has happened to my life? I've gone from doing my own thing to dealing with two hormonal chicks in the space of a few goddamn weeks. Maybe it's time to move on to the next spot. Now, even that's a record for me.

"Jensen. You here?" I'm siting at the kitchen table waiting for Minnie to get off the phone, when I hear Boyd's voice booming through the house. His timing is perfect as I'm about to go coo-coo sat her with *Miss fucking Cupid*. All she's harped on about this morning is how I need to speak to Anna, let her know how I feel, and how Minnie and Darcie were just a bunch of misunderstandings. I don't need to listen to Minnie; I don't need to say shit. By the looks of things, she's already made her assumptions of me crystal clear and that's fine by me. Plus, she regrets what happened between us anyway, so what's the fucking point?

"Yeah, in here." I shout out from the kitchen.

"What happened?" He asks. "I've been waiting for you all morning and you're not picking up on your phone."

"Back up a bit, man. Why were you

waiting for me?" Boyd looks at me as if I have lost my mind. I have no fucking clue what he's trying to tell me, all I can see is his fucking eyebrows jumping up and down as if he can suddenly talk to me in a secret language. "Give me a goddamn clue, then."

"We were supposed to drive and see Mitchell, remember?" It takes a couple of seconds for his words to sink in. Fuck, now I remember. I glance at the clock and I know instantly that we're never going to make it on time now. Even if Boyd put his foot down, visiting would be over. He's going to hit the roof when I don't show and it's not as if I can call him to tell him either. Fuck, fuck, fuck.

"What's that about Mitchell?" Minnie appears next to us in the kitchen and Boyd pales instantly. Today is just going from bad to fucking worse with each passing second.

"Jensen was..." He starts, but quickly stumbles. It fucking serves him right for dropping me in this shit in the first place.

"I was gonna to try and find a way to see if you could go and visit him." I lie, eager to stop Boyd from dropping both me and Mitchell in the shit with Minnie."

"Oh yeah? You never said last night." Sounding surprised, a smile graces her small mouth, which makes me feel worse for lying to her.

"It's because of last night. I'm not gonna lie to you Min, it killed me seeing you so upset, so I called Boyd to see if I could pull in a favour, but there's no way that we'll get there on time to see him. Sorry Min. I promise I'll speak to him and see what I can do."

"Okay, and thanks for doing this J, it means a lot. You know that right?" She watches me with uncertainty written across her face. If she knew I was going to see him without her, she'd have my balls on a platter and that isn't something I fancy anytime soon.

ANNA

I haven't seen Jensen since our heated blow out yesterday morning, and I'm absolutely fine with that. I'm surprised by how I've dealt with the whole situation too. The house has felt much calmer without him here, and it's given me some much needed thinking space. I try to stop my mind from wandering when it comes to his whereabouts though. I guess that's really none of my business, yet, I can't stop the thought of him with someone else and it fills me with nausea. I haven't been rota'd on at Temptation either, so I haven't had to face Darcie or Joey recently and for that I'm thankful. Maybe if I'd had to work with them yesterday, then I wouldn't have been able to hold back with my opinions, but now that I've had time to think, and to calm myself down, I've realised that it isn't my place to interfere with their private lives. What they do and who they sleep with is completely up to them and no one else. The best thing I can do; is to stay far, far away from it all, physically and emotionally.

I sometimes wish that my life had taken a completely different direction, but as a teenager, sometimes you can't help but follow the crowd; just to make sure that you fit in. If only I'd just listened to everyone at the beginning, then maybe I'd still be at home, living my happy, every day to day life and I would never have met Jensen. What did I know? I thought I knew everything back then. I had my friends, my family and soon I had a boyfriend who loved me and would do anything for me. I had heaps of friends and we always made sure that we had a great time. Every day was full of life and laughter and we always made sure that we were there for each other, no matter what. Sure, as we grew older, most of them dabbled in drugs from time to time, but I preferred to stay away from taking them, and thankfully everyone respected my decision. I decided that if they wanted to do stuff like that, then it was on their head and their head alone if anything bad were to come of it. It wasn't long when I started to notice small changes happening within our circle. The girls, who I was really close to at the time, started to get distant and sometimes I wouldn't see them for weeks on end. I often wondered if it was me and if I'd done something to upset them.

"Don't be so paranoid." They'd say to me, whenever I expressed my concern over their well-being. *"We can't be with you all the time Anna. Just relax and stop over thinking things, you'll make yourself ill."*

As time went on, I'd see them less and less and Dom also became quite distant too and that hurt me the most. It was something that he'd never done before. No matter what he had going on his life, he always put me first and I found the change hard to handle. I suddenly found myself very confused and very lonely. I was certain he was sleeping with one of my friends and it caused so much tension between us. The arguments and the fights were horrible and I started to blame myself and wondered how it all went so wrong so fast. It eventually got that bad, that we almost split up over it a few times, and that broke my heart into a million pieces. Dom was all I had ever known, all I ever wanted to know. He just didn't seem to get it. He couldn't understand why I'd be the one who was left heartbroken because somehow, I knew I was losing the man that I loved and I didn't even know why, or how to stop it from happening. I was desperate to get his attention on *me* again. I craved for him to care about me the way he used to do. I wanted to feel worshipped, just like the way he used to make me feel; so I started dressing older than my years, and wearing more make-up in the hope that he would finally *see* me again, and it worked for a short while. Dom and I were happy again and nothing could come between us. He showered me with extravagant gifts and I showered him with love and affection. I was finally happy in myself again and I felt utterly untouchable when I was with him. Looking back, I guess that's what immaturity does to you. A lesson; that I learned only too well.

It didn't help our relationship, that my dad hated Dom with a passion. I struggled to understand why he wouldn't approve of him and our relationship. All I wanted, was for my dad to be happy for me; to see that I had someone who really loved me and who would care for me, no matter what, but he just couldn't see it. By the time I was turning twenty-one, Dom and I had been together for almost three years and in my head we were destined to be together forever. All we needed to do now was get married and create some babies. You couldn't get any more perfect than that. Could you?

"Move in with me Anna? That way no one can come between us. It will be just you and me against the world, baby."

"You really mean that?" I asked him, with love hammering so hard in my chest, that I actually thought it would combust. Every day I asked myself how I got so lucky to end up with him. Sure, he could be an absolute bastard at times; and a dangerous bastard at that, when it came to other people that fucked him over; but with me, I was his princess and he would do anything for me to make me happy.

"Of course I mean it. I love you Anna, and I don't see why we shouldn't be together all the time. What d'ya say?"

"Yes, oh my god, of course I will."

The first six months in our new home were amazing. Honestly, it was like something out of the movies. I used to play the happy little housewife, making sure all the chores were done and that Dom had a hot, homemade meal on the table when he got home, while he went out and provided for us. I had no reason to question what he was doing and we were happy, so, so happy. As I look back, in that six months, I genuinely believe that we were the happiest that we had ever been and blissfully in love, but then something changed. I didn't know what it was, but he just switched. Dominic just wasn't acting his usual happy self towards me anymore. Gone was my happy-go-lucky, loveable boyfriend and instead I was met every day with a stressed out man who very rarely decided to come home. When he did come home, I tried everything to keep the connection going between us. Desperate, to keep our relationship alive. He no longer confided in me and he'd brush off my sexual advances unless he wanted to get his leg over, and even then the intimacy seemed to have vanished. All I could do was Lay there as he panted above me until he was satisfied, without a care in the world about my needs or feelings. I asked him countless times if he was seeing someone else, and although he swore he wasn't, I just didn't believe him. He'd tell me he loved me when I got upset, or if I asked too many questions in a bid to keep me quiet, and blindly, I believed him. I listened to his every word, stupidly believing that it could only get better and that this was a just a little blip in our relationship. Every couple had them didn't they? He really could do no wrong in my eyes and god forbid anyone else who tried to tell me otherwise.

"Have you calmed down now?" I'm pulled from my past at the sound of Jensen's voice. As I look up, I realise just how much I have missed seeing him when he's stood right in front of me. Tall, dark and sexy as hell, dripping in sweat, which I'm guessing is from a run.

"Have you stopped being a twat?" I ask, far from ready to play nice with him.

"In your eyes I'll always be a twat, so is there really any point in answering that question?" He laughs as he pulls a dining chair out opposite me. The night we spent together flickers through my mind and my face heats up from the vivid memories.

"Where've you been?" I ask him and a sense of déjà vu overcomes me as I wait for his answer. "*Jensen isn't Dominic, Anna.*" I tell myself and I could slap myself for comparing the two of them. I don't want to put anyone into the same category as Dominic. Ever. No one can ever be as vile as that piece of scum.

"Honestly? I thought I'd give you some space. I realised that maybe this is all a bit too much for you, having me here."

"It's not too much, Jensen. It was a shock, but you bought this place fair and square and you're letting me stay here, so who am I to complain, really?"

"I didn't mean that Anna. I meant what happened the other night..."

"What about it? There's nothing to say." My defences instantly shoot up. Why, oh, why does he have to bring this up now? Does he want to humiliate me even more, knowing that I'm a just a tiny notch against the many others that he's racked up on his bedpost.

"No? I think there is. Why do you act like you don't care? Granted, it was a shag, a pretty memorable one at that, but still a shag. If you don't want it to be more than that, then fine; but why are you so against everything?"

I watch him sitting in front of me, all calm and collected and looking sexy as hell, but every bone in my body is telling me to stay away from him. I know that he's not Dominic, but he's the same kind of guy. He's dangerous and obnoxious and, shit I can't even look at him and think straight. It's impossible.

"I'm not against everything, Jensen. Like I said the other day, you can sleep with who you want." My voice betrays me, as I say those words in a high pitched squeal.

"I know, but why are you so uptight about it? I need you to help me out here, Anna. I'm trying my goddamn hardest to figure you out and you're holding all these barriers up, and I just don't know why."

"Jensen, I don't know about you, but for me, if I've just slept with someone; whether it was a mistake or not, I wouldn't be able to sleep with someone else, let alone two other people in a twenty-four hour period."

"What the fuck are you talking about?" Confusion is written all over his face now.

"What am I talking about? What are you, crazy? Forget it, it doesn't matter anyway." It's pointless continuing this conversation, because it's only going to get heated. We clash, there's no denying it and it's easier for us both if we just drop it.

"To hell it doesn't matter." He shouts and I can see that he's getting angry and frustrated with me. "If it's bothering you, then it matters to *me*. So tell me, what the fuck are you talking about?"

I let out a sigh, not sure where I'm going to start. I'm going to sound like a petty fucking teenager, but the way he's glowering at me, he's making it pretty clear that none of us are going to be leaving this room until I give him an explanation. "The morning after, well, I woke up and you were gone. I'm not gonna lie to you, I was glad that you weren't around. It meant that I didn't need to face you, or talk about it, and that way I could tell myself that it didn't happen. Then when I arrived at the bar, I came to talk to you, but you and Darcie were all over each other like the fucking plague, and that hurt Jensen. I don't know why, because I can't stand you at the best of times, but to know you were in my bed with me, only a few hours before; it fucking hurt. I'm not a slut Jensen, and I don't usually do what I did. I knew right in that moment that I was right to put it down as a mistake. A mistake, that I wasn't going to repeat again. So then imagine my surprise when I got home later that night, to see you coming down the stairs, half naked, only to hear another female voice floating around the house; only to then find you in a nice cosy embrace with her on the sofa the next morning." Yeah, I definitely just came across as a whiney teenager, but it's out there; just like he wanted.

"Okay... So I understand where you're coming from, but you've got it all wrong. So, so, fucking wrong." He's actually smiling at me as he says this.

"I'm glad you find this all highly amusing. Looks like you've had your fun, so how about we forget that it ever happened?" I ask him on a plea, hoping he'll agree with me, but this is Jensen that we're talking about here.

"You think I don't want to? You think I haven't fucking tried? Every second of every goddamn day, all I can see is your face and all I can hear in my head is that smart fucking mouth of yours. You drive me fucking crazy and it's not something that I'm used to okay. This isn't easy for me Anna."

I have nothing to say to him. All I can do is sit here and listen to the bullshit that's coming out of his mouth. I begin to wonder how many times he's spouted these lines so that he can get another leg over.

"It might have been a *mistake* for you, but it wasn't for me. I wasn't there when you woke up, because I didn't know what you would say. I actually *cared* about how you would react and I didn't want to upset you, and for me, that isn't something that usually happens. I watched you fucking sleep for hours, for god's sake." He pauses and taps his fingers lightly against the antique table before continuing. "What you saw with Darcie was almost right. We go back a long time and yeah, we've had our fair share of fun with each other along the way. I wanted to forget about you. I needed to get you out of my mind, even if it was for a little while, so I decided that the best way to do that was to go back to what I know; by distracting myself with her. I tried, but I couldn't do it. Fucking hell, it just didn't feel right. It's as if my body knew that she wasn't you. Me, and Darcie have never had that problem before, so I shrugged it off and told her maybe some other time."

I continue to sit in silence, as I listen to his confession. I feel slightly sick, listening to how much detail he is going in to. I'll never be able to prove if what he's saying is true, but why should I believe him? "Why are you telling me this Jensen?"

"Why am I telling you this? I'm telling you this because I'm not the heartless bastard, that you think I am. When it comes to you, I wish I was. It would be so much easier to dislike you, but all I can think about is you, how your warm body feels pressed against mine and how you feel underneath me; but you're not prepared to meet me halfway, so what's the fucking point?" He pushes himself back and stands up before giving me one last glance before turning to leave. Talk about a serious case of head-fuck. What am I supposed to do with that information anyway? *Way to go Anna, you've gone and fucked up once again.*

JENSEN

I've laid my cards on the table. I swallowed my pride and told Anna exactly how I feel. Fuck me; Minnie would be so goddamn proud of me right now. I don't know what I expected her to say, but to watch her sit there in silence, told me that I was wasting my fucking time anyway. At least now she knows that for me, it wasn't a casual lay. I can't believe she thought I'd slept with Darcie and Minnie too. I have my fair share of fun, sure; but even that's taking it a bit too fucking far. I know she's still sat in the kitchen, as I've not heard her move, but I can't just sit there and pour my heart out to her. I've said my piece and that's all she's going to get. It's up to her what she does with it.

"Hey, it's me." Boyd's voice greets me on the other end of the line.

"Yo man, what's up?" I hope he isn't in one of his fucked up, giddy moods today, because I don't think I can deal with it today.

"I need to talk to you as soon as possible. I've woken up to a message from Mitchell this morning. Where can we meet?"

"Whoa, back up a bit. What's Mitchell doing calling you instead of me?" Mitchell's my fucking brother, so what's he doing calling Boyd? If he needs something, then he calls me, he's always called me. Something doesn't sound right here, and I need to know what it is.

"Mitchell knows that Minnie's been back on the scene and didn't want to call you in case she was there or something. Make sense now?"

"Yeah, yeah it does. I haven't told him that Minnie's here though. He's gonna go crazy knowing that she's here." How does he even know that she's in Boston?

"Listen, I'm on my way and we can discuss it then."

"Yo, Min. What you doing today?" I need to try and make her leave the house without her getting suspicious. Whatever Boyd tells me, clearly isn't meant for anyone else, otherwise Mitchell would have called me direct. Well, at least that's what I'm hoping anyway. He's never had an issue with Minnie coming over in the past, so I don't see why he should start now. Plus, she's only just arrived here.

"I'm gonna head out to the shops in a little bit, why, you need some stuff?"

"I was just wondering. I'm gonna have to head out myself soon and I don't know how long I'll be. Just got some errands to run with Boyd, you know how he is, he's worse than a kid if there's no one by his side to hold his hand." I hate lying to her. She's like the big sister that I never had, so getting rid of her intentionally isn't something that I want to do. Shit, it's something that I wouldn't do at all, but Mitchell's keeping her out of this for a reason.

"Sure thing. Let me get ready and then I'll be out of your hair."

Boyd arrives around ten minutes after Minnie left and he looks frantic as hell. His face is flushed, and he's breathing as if he's been chased by the cop's all the way here. I wait until he's sat in the chair before I start my interrogation.

"What's happening? Why'd Mitchell call? Why do you look so worked up?"

"Something's not right J. Mitchell didn't sound happy, at all."

"What did he say?" How hard can it be to get to the goddamn point of the phone call?

"Something about some guy that you two were talking about when he saw you last. He wants you to keep a look out for him or something. Apparently he's floating around this area, but no one knows what for. Mitchell thinks something dodgy's going on, but he can't put his finger on it."

"Right, well that makes no fucking sense to me. We spoke about all sorts while I was there. I didn't know I was supposed to fucking memorise everything. Why couldn't he just tell me?" As much as I appreciate having Boyd in my life, he's pointless when comes to relaying information and fucking Mitchell knows it too. I guess all I can do is sit back and hope that he calls me or I get to go and see him, soon. I can't be any help to him, if I don't have the right information to go off.

"I thought it was cryptic too, but then again, he could have been around anyone and didn't want them overhearing. I would have asked him for some more info, J; but you know how he gets."

"Yeah I guess. There's not much I can do with that anyway. We'll just have to sit tight and hope we hear something else from him, and if he calls you; you tell him to fucking call me, you got it?"

Temptation is quite lively when I arrive, which is always a good sign; especially for my pockets. I'm glad this place has its own regulars. It makes it feel welcoming. There's nothing worse than running a joint that's like a fucking ghost town. I've been there and it's fucking shit. Not exactly something to make me stay around. My eyes fall on Anna as I push my way through the crowds and I give her a slight nod. I'm done with the awkwardness around us. We either decide to get on, or we only talk when we need to. I've said my piece and she knows where she stands. The balls firmly in her court if she decides to act on anything that I've said. I reach the office and I can hear giggling coming from inside. Who the fuck's in my office? Pushing the door open, I find Joey and Darcie pressed up against the wall, having a damn good time by the looks of things. Joey's pants are halfway down his legs, and Darcie as usual is wearing next to nothing.

"Break it up." I shout as I slam the door open wide. "I said break it fucking up. Ain't nobody screwing on my watch. You wanna get you're dick wet, pal?" I say as I look at Joey. "Then make your fucking way to the local parlour and not with my staff."

"Jensen, get your fucking panties out of your arse. It's only a bit of fun; you remember what that is, right?" Darcie looks at me with a mischievous smile plastered across her ruby red lips. Sure I know what fun is alright and I remember how those lips feel against my cock; but she ain't got shit on Anna.

"You." I shout at Joey. "Get the fuck out of here while you've still got a dick." Darcie can fuck who she wants, but I ain't having no one else's bodily fluids in my office but my own. It's fucking disrespectful. "I didn't hire you to sleep with the staff, did I?"

"No, however it's one of those fabulous

perks of the job. C'mon Jensen. What's up with you? You're so uptight all the time, recently. What's wrong? You used to be so laid back."

I know she's right but I'm not going to admit it. "I've got a lot going on right now Darce, don't take it personally."

"Yeah, how about I help you relive some of that tension? You know you'll feel better." She croons at me. Usually my pants would have been at my ankles by now, but I just can't do it.

"Nah, I'm good. I just need to get cracking with this shit that's quickly piling up. It's getting busy out there right now, maybe you should go and give lover boy a hand, and I don't mean down his fucking pants either, you hear me?"

"Are you jealous that he wants my attention, J?" I lift my eyes up to meet hers, and as I look at her, I feel no attraction there whatsoever. Not like I used to.

"No, not one little bit Darce." I've never felt more sure, about anything before, but as I look at her, I can see all we were good for was a dynamite fuck. Or at least that's what I thought a dynamite fuck was, but I didn't know shit until I'd experienced that with Anna.

"Okay. Well just remember it's your loss sunshine. That prude in there isn't gonna make you happy, you know that right?"

"You know shit about Anna, so watch your fucking mouth." I snap and the words are out of my mouth before I can stop them. I don't give a shit how long I've known Darcie, but I won't have her bad mouthing Anna.

"And there it is. Jensen Blake's finally got it bad for some chick. I never thought I'd see the day." She slaps me hard on the shoulder before laughing smugly at me.

"Get the fuck out of here, before I fire your arse."

"Yes, Boss."

ANNA

I didn't think it'd be long before Joey came running out of the office with his tail between his legs. I so wish I could have been a fly on the wall when Jensen walked into that office. Of course, I already knew what was going on, but it's not my job to keep the staff under control. Not anymore, anyway. Jensen has made it pretty clear who is boss around here, so it's his problem if he's got uncontrollable staffing issues. Not long after, Darcie leaves the office and throws me a fowl look. I have no idea what her problem is, but if she wants to play games, then that's fine by me.

"You want to watch that one." I say to Joe as he comes up behind me at the bar.

"Who Darcie? Are you shitting me? She's a gem that girl, a real rare find." Oh boy, he's got it so, so bad. He can't even see how much she is taking him for a ride.

"Well, don't say I didn't warn you Joe. I don't like her, there's something about her that's just, off. I reckon she'd stab you in the back the minute that she would benefit from it. All I'm saying is; just don't fall too deep, okay."

"It's just a bit of fun Anna. I keep telling you, maybe you should try it. Get some fun in your life, and live a little, instead of brooding over that secretive past of yours."

"Joey baby, could you give me a hand with this?" I look over and see that Darcie is bent over the bar, seductively trying to grab a bottle, yet only managing to look even more of a slut in the process, proving that the impossible is possible. This woman has no fucking shame whatsoever and how Jensen, or Joey could even go there is beyond me. Joey gives me a wink, and a quick pat to the shoulder before making his way over to her like a love struck little puppy and it's all a little bit sickening, but all I can do is watch him walk way. I've tried to warn him, but maybe he'll need to lean the hard way for a change.

"Hey lady. I'll have a beer when you're ready."

"Oh yeah? You want to use some manners with that?" I ask the man stood before me. He's tall, with dark blonde hair and piercing green eyes. I'd be lying if I said he wasn't beautiful. Something about him just draws me in instantly. He's no Jensen, but he's attractive none the less.

"How about I give you my number, instead. Then I could show you just how good my manners can be?" All of his beauty suddenly vanishes with that comment and all I see is another average sleaze ball stood in front of me, out to get a quick lay.

"Thanks, but I'm good." I laugh, wondering what chat up line he's going to use next. I pour his beer and I can feel his intense gaze lingering on me. Working in this place, I'm used to the come-ons and chat up lines from the regulars, but I've not seen this guy in here before. Maybe he's one of Jensen's pals. I don't see any tatts on him and, I know I shouldn't stereotype, but he just doesn't look like he'd fit in with Jensen's crowd.

"Go on sweetheart, what harm can it do? You might even find that I'm the *one*." He smiles at me, trying to persuade me to give in." How about I give you my number and it's up to you if you call me. No pressure, if you don't call, then you don't call. The ball will be solely in your court, now you can't say fairer than that."

Smiling politely at him, I decline his offer once again and hand over his beer. He is pretty hot though, but no way in hell will I be ringing a stranger to meet up with him. I'm not that fucking crazy. This guy could be anyone and the last thing I want is certain people finding out that I'm here. Too many innocent people could get hurt.

"Well, my names Jed, you know, just in case you change your mind, and here's my number." He places a card on the bar and leans over slightly, gripping my hand in his, while trying to hold my neck with the other to pull me in. "You're pretty fucking beautiful, you know that?" I'm suddenly way out of my comfort zone here and he needs to quickly back off.

"Everything alright here, mate?" Jed quickly pulls back at the sound of Jensen's voice, and by his tone, I would too.

"Yeah, I was just appreciating this beautiful lady here. Is that a problem?"

"You bet it is. Go take your drink and admire her from afar, because that's as close as you'll ever fucking get." I don't know whether I should be thankful that Jensen came to my rescue, or pissed off at him for interfering. I could have had that under control and I sure as hell don't need him to fight my battles for me. I've managed so far in life already without him. "You okay?" He asks as soon as Jed is out of ear shot. His eyes search my face, looking for any sign that Jed hurt me, probably so he can find an excuse to go and smash his face in.

"Yeah, thanks." I look at him and smile thankfully, deciding to give him the benefit of the doubt that he was just being protective over his staff. So why does he look so furious? Anyone would think that he'd been threatened by the way he's acting. His body is tense and his breathing is laboured, even though I can tell that he's trying his damned hardest to hide it.

The bar is the busiest that I have seen it in a while and it doesn't skip my attention that Jensen serves every, single male who comes up to get a drink and leaves all the women to the rest of us. Granted there are more women than men here tonight, but I don't think for a second that what he's doing is a coincidence.

"What's your problem?" I ask, as soon as the bar has quietened down a little. He looks at me, yet says nothing. "Come on Jensen. I'm not in the mood to play games tonight."

"No? I'm sure I could think of a few that you'd like." He flashes me his devilish grin and I can't help but smile back at him.

"What are you doing out here? You're normally holed up in your man space, not out here, with us peasants."

"What? Am I not allowed to pull my finger out now?

"Sure you can. Your can do whatever you want, but don't think that it's gone unnoticed that you've kept me away from serving the guys."

"Listen, I'm not going to sit back and watch you get ogled by a bunch of low life's, Anna."

"How the hell do you know if he's a low life? For all you know, I could have known that guy already." His face changes as a *"Do you think I was born yesterday?"* look spreads across his face. "So you're telling me that I'm only allowed to serve women from now on?"

"I'm keeping an eye on my staff. Is that a

problem?" He dares me to argue with him and I really want to. I've told him before that I won't put up with him telling me what to do, and just as I'm about to tell him what I really think of him and his rules, Darcie steps in between us.

"Hey J, you mind if me and Joey take off now that it's quiet? I wouldn't ask usually but we've got some unfinished business. You know how it is." She trails her finger across his chest, flirting with him and it only makes her look cheap. Ugh, she makes me physically sick.

"Do what the fuck you want Darce, just make sure you're on time for your shift tomorrow." He pulls his head away from her and serves the guy who's just appeared, and he looks so pissed off. Is he pissed because Darcie is going home with Joey tonight, and not him?

"He's way out of your league sweetheart." She smiles ever so sweetly at me, but I can see a pool of pure jealousy simmering in her eyes as she looks me up and down. "I wouldn't bother, unless you've got balls made of steel."

"You ain't got a fucking clue what I'm made of, *Darce."* I mimic, "But thanks for the heads up."

It's gone two in the morning by the time Jensen and I have managed to remove everyone from the bar. The last few hours were quiet, that's probably due to the fact that most of the punters had drank more than they could handle and were falling asleep, hidden in the corners and even under the tables. I noticed Jed was still lingering in the crowd, but he didn't bother either of us again, since Jensen had warned him off earlier.

"You want a drink?" Jensen asks me, already pouring himself one and pauses over the second glass, waiting for my reply.

"I think I'll pass. You and I don't mix that well, especially when alcohol's involved on my part, do we?" I throw my towel down and hop on to the barstool to relieve my tired feet. Maybe I should keep a pair of flats behind the bar for when I'm working, because now I'm paying for wearing those goddamn heels.

"Oh I wouldn't say that. I think you're pretty naughty when you've had a drink, but then you could be exactly the same sober. I guess I'll never find out."

"Why did you interfere before with that guy?" It's been bugging me all night and the more I think about it, the more it looks like he was marking his territory.

"You okay with random guys hitting on you, 'cos I sure aint." He knocks back his drink and pours another one and chases it down instantly with another shot.

"Jensen, I work in a bar. Guys hit on girls all the time. It's only like some girl hitting on you, or that guy hitting in Darcie."

"I couldn't give a toss who hits on Darcie. Darcie isn't *you*; do you not get that yet? I don't like men hitting on you, full fucking stop okay. It makes me feel…"

"Jensen, you can't…"

"Don't tell me what to do Anna. I never fucking asked for this. You've been running through my head since I first walked into this place and no matter what I do, I can't get you out of it. It's driving me goddamn crazy."

I grab the bottle from his hands and pour myself a drink. It looks like I'm going to need a few of these to get through this conversation with him. "Oh, I know the feeling, believe me."

"Then what's your problem? Why are you doing everything you can to push me away? Shit Anna, I'm not saying let's run off and get married, but we could at least have some fun, explore this attraction between us and see what happens."

"I can't do it Jensen. Shit, it's too long to explain, but I won't put myself through anything that I've already been through before. There is no way that I'm signing myself up for that, ever again." God that sounds so pathetic when I say it out loud. There's no way that he'd understand anyway, so what's the point in trying to explain?

"You're holding back, and denying yourself, because of something that happened to you? Tell me what it was and maybe I'll understand you better. If I need to approach you with caution, then tell me. If I'm doing something that hurts you, then tell me. How hard can it be to fucking communicate? We live together for god's sake."

"Like I said, it's a long story and not worth getting into. The bottom line is, I'm not prepared to be used for sex Jensen. I won't be your go to girl when you feel horny. There's no way in hell that I'd be comfortable with that."

"A compromise; then?" He asks with a glint of danger in his eyes.

"What do you mean?" I ask, uncertain of where this is going, and unsure if I really want to know.

"You lay your cards out, here and now, about what you do want, and I'll see if it's worth a compromise, and then I'll do the same. What do you say?" Wow. He's actually being serious here too. I just don't understand why he wants me?

"I physically can't sleep with someone that I don't have feelings for, I'm just not built that way, and I don't want to feel anything for anyone at the moment. It's too much, too soon." Jensen's quiet for a while, rolling his empty glass around in his palms as he takes in what I've just said. Suddenly he gets up and walks in the opposite direction. "What..." I start but before I can continue, he turns back around and I fell his lips against mine, still laced with alcohol, and I can't help but reciprocate his actions.

"But you already have feelings for me. That's one hurdle out of the way, huh?" He says in between kisses.

"I don't want to have feelings for you. I can't have feelings for you, Jensen." I pull back from him so that I can look him straight in the eye. "Everything that I have built up since I have been here, is about to be ruined because of you, and I don't know if I can let that happen. I can't just let you in, just for you to destroy me further on down the line." I know I don't sound as convincing as I should, but when he's near me like this, with his heart hammering against mine, all I want is for him to touch me the way he did the other night, and I hate myself for it, I bloody hate him for it too.

"It sounds like you already have to me. Don't sweat it; just follow your heart and not your head." That's fucking easy for him to say, seeing as though his feelings are positioned firmly between those powerful thighs. I allow him to pull me in once again and I know, somewhere, deep down, that I will live to regret this. I've been fighting him for what feels like forever and I just can't do it anymore. The feel of him this close to me is burning away any brain cells and common sense that I have left. I feel my feet lift the ground, as he lifts me up in his arms and places me ever so gently on the bar. His hooded eyes have my body turning to liquid as he looks at me, undressing me once again with his eyes. My breathing picks up and I wish that I could resist him, but the harder I try, the harder I fail.

"I like it when you play nice, Anna." His voice is husky and deep, and vibrates against my skin as he slowly and teasingly places small kisses on my calf, working his way up towards the centre of my body. My head falls back on a soft whimper, and I feel him chuckle, a soft, boyish chuckle at my weakness. I can't take this anymore, I'm sure he takes his sweet time with me to see how far he can push me. Well not this time, pal. I fist my hands and pull him up so that I can feel his hard body against mine. I don't need slow. I don't need to be teased, what I need is for Jensen to be inside me, now.

"What's the rush? I want to explore every fucking inch of you, I want to experience every fucking inch of you." His thumb finds its way inside my panties and presses ever so perfectly on my sweet spot, and then he slowly moves away, with his cocky grin dancing on his lips. My hips buckle under his touch, leaving me desperate for more of him, and then I'm left feeling empty as he draws back. "I can keep doing this all night, until you quit rushing, Anna. I have no problem bringing you as close to the edge as possible, just to pull you right back to the start."

JENSEN

When I saw that douche hitting on Anna from the CCTV in the office, I felt like my head was going to explode. To witness another guy checking her out bothered me. It bothered me more than I'll ever like to admit and before I knew it, I was out of that door, desperate to get him away from her. I've never experienced anything fucking like it before. I guess people may call it jealously, but what would I know? I've never cared enough about someone to feel that way, but I know that I don't ever want to feel that way again. All I could see was red, and if he wasn't prepared to back the fuck away from her, then he would have left this bar minus his teeth. Now, I stand here with her nestled perfectly in between my thighs, pulling her closer to me and in this moment, there is nowhere else that I would rather be. Fucking hell, I'm hooked. Anna Jameson is about to turn me into one of those, pussy whipped guys that I've spent most of my life taking the fucking piss out of.

"You want to head home?" I ask her, pulling her face up from where it's resting on my shoulder, as she comes down from the mighty high that she's just experienced. Her eyes are mixed with pure lust, yet somewhere deep within them is a raw sadness. "What's wrong?"

"I'm fine. I'm just confused as hell. I didn't set out to want this, Jensen. I tried everything I could to stay away from you, but I can't do it. You're the type of guy that I've been trying to avoid. I swore to myself that I wouldn't fall into this kind of trap again. I guess it's easier said than done, when I see you every day, huh?"

"You and me both. I'm not going to lie to you, but after last time I thought I'd be able to get you out of my system, but it only made me want you more, need you more. So, am I pushing my luck if I ask if you're done with pushing me away, or is that asking for too much?" I breathe a sigh if relief when I get a small laugh from her. Finally, she's warming towards me, *to us*. "Come on, let's get you home."

"How do?" Anna walks into the kitchen wearing nothing other than my t-shirt from last night, and my balls ache at the sight of her. Hot damn, that chick is smoking. What did I do to get this lucky? If I ever see Holly again, I'm going to have to repay her for this little gem of a cousin of hers, big time.

"Hey you. You're up early." I know what she's thinking instantly, and I don't want any bad vibes between us, not now that we finally seem to be able to hold a conversation without her storming out on me.

"I don't sleep much, I never have. If you're wondering why I wasn't with you when you woke up, it's because I didn't know how you'd react. I don't feel like a repeat of last time, you know?"

"Right." Her tone is flat and I can almost feel her pulling back from me.

"Hey, it's not because I didn't want to be there, believe me, there's nowhere else that I would rather be. I just didn't know how you'd feel about waking up with me, that's all."

"I would have been fine with it, honestly. It would have been nice to see you, to feel you next to me, I guess."

"Yeah? Well that's pretty good to know for next time." I can't help the smile that appears on my face. This girl, as smart as that mouth of hers is, she's pretty fucking awesome.

"Next time? You're pretty sure of yourself aren't you?"

Standing up and walking towards her, I cup her face in my hands. "You better believe it; I'm far from done with you." With a swift move of my hand, I pull her up against me and feel a thrill of pure satisfaction at the moan that falls from her lips. Her hands are soon on my body as she explores lightly with the tips of her fingers and it feels so fucking good. "How about we take this back upstairs? Let me make up for my no show, this morning?"

"Oh, excuse me children. Sorry to break up the party." I throw my head back in despair at the sound of that voice. Why now? For fuck sake.

"Minnie, what the fuck are you doing here? You can't just turn up and walk into someone's house, uninvited. That shit doesn't rest easy with me, and you fucking know it."

"Whoa. I'm sorry." She holds both of her hands up and pouts slightly in our direction, while I do my best to shield Anna from Minnie's curious gaze. Ain't no one but me seeing what my shirts barely covering on her body.

"Well what do you want? Can't you see I'm in the middle of something here?"

"I'm just gonna go get dressed, anyway." Anna whispers from behind me. She quickly manoeuvres around me and makes a run for it towards the stairs. Before she falls out of my line of vision, I can see that her face is bright red from embarrassment.

"I could actually kill you right now Min. Do you know that? This better be fucking important."

"It's great to see you too J. I'm glad that you finally saw sense and got it on with your hot roomie. I gotta admit, she's certainly something."

"What do you want?" I say again. I can feel myself getting more and more angry with each second that passing by. She's keeping me from Anna, and that makes pisses me off.

"Mitchell called me." She says with a full on smile plastered across her face. "I actually got to have a full blown conversation with him J, and it felt so good."

"And...?" I ask. I know that I should be happy for her, shit she's been waiting for this call for months, but I just can't find it in me to share her enjoyment. My enjoyment is currently upstairs, putting clothes on that fine arse body, that I so desperately want to keep bare.

"He's coming home J. I'm so fucking happy. I'm sorry for barging in on you like a mad woman, but I needed to tell someone, you know? You were the only person I knew who cares about him as much as me."

I feel bad raining on her parade, but she's just broke up what was set to be a magical morning. "Could you not have called, or something? You know give me a heads up or something? Jeez Minnie, do you know how bad you've messed up my morning?"

"Quit your moaning dude, I'm sure she'll be ready and waiting for you once I'm gone. But for now, I need you with me."

"Actually, I've got to head out for a little while, but I'll be back later." She looks at Minnie in embarrassment and I really want to make pay Minnie pay for making Anna feel so uncomfortable.

"You want a ride?" I ask, hoping that she'll say yes and then I can spend some more time with her.

"I'm good, but I'll call you later, okay?"

"Sure thing." My chest instantly deflates in defeat as I watch her walk away from me. I know it's weird, but every time I watch her walk away from me, I fear that she won't come back, and it's starting to scare the living shit out of me.

Turning back around, I find Minnie seated at the table, helping herself to the freshly brewed coffee. She looks up at me as I sit down and smiles apologetically at me.

"Hey, have you spoken to Mitchell yet? He seems pretty concerned about some guy. I can't remember his name though and I wondered if you knew anything about it? He sounded pretty worried about it, to be honest."

"I haven't got a clue what he's going on about it, but I know Mitchell and if he's that concerned and he wants me to know about it, then he'll call me."

ANNA

Talk about embarrassing. Had she walked in more than five minutes later, it's likely that she would have found me spread out underneath Jensen, having the time of my life. Why the hell didn't he have the door locked? That's something that I'm going to have to talk to him about. I need to have that door locked at all times otherwise I'll have a mental fucking breakdown, worried about what could happen. Yes, it's highly unlikely, but you never know if you're safe anywhere. Especially me. Ever since I moved in with Holly, that door has always been locked and you could only get in if you had a key. Shit, was it open all night? I dread to think what could have happened if he'd come looking for me and found Jensen and I in that embrace. Sure, Jensen's a big guy, and I'm pretty sure that he can look after himself, but I'd hate anything bad to happen to him because of me and my stupid mistakes. The thought of anything bad happening to Jensen causes a sudden dull ache to penetrate my chest and it frightens the crap out of me.

I pull up into the parking lot where I take my class. It's not overly large, but it's big enough to accommodate a hundred or so people, and the courses range from English, to science, to martial arts. English was the first choice I made, and thankfully I got a place. I know for a fact that I wouldn't have stuck to any of the other courses. I don't even need to be here today, but after Minnie's dramatic entrance this morning, I thought the library would be the best place to come and get my head down. A little bit of extra revision never hurt anyone either. Two birds with one stone, and all that. As I get closer to the entrance, I see a figure stood right outside the doors. I can't make out their face due to a hood concealing them. I automatically panic and it takes me a few minutes to calm myself down. I must look like a right weirdo, stood in the middle of the parking lot, standing still, gazing around me. *"It's probably someone here about a course, or maybe halfway through their course."* I think to myself. I cautiously put one foot in front of the other and make my way to the entrance, knowing that if I loiter around much longer, it will only cause unwanted attention around me. "Hey. Remember me?" He asks as I approach the doors. Oh fucking great. Now I've got to deal with this arsehole while I'm here too.

"Hey, what are you doing here?" I don't really want to encourage him by giving him an answer, but I've always been brought up to be polite to people.

"Had your boyfriend stayed out of our little conversation, I could have told you that I'm new in town and I was keen to make some friends while I'm here. Is that so bad?" He shrugs his shoulders at me, and now I feel bad for Jensen butting in the way he did.

"You studying here? Or are you following me?"

"Nah, I'm just checking out stuff to keep me entertained while I'm here, you know? I don't fancy that thing called boredom setting in."

"Yeah, I completely get that." What are these words that are coming out of my mouth? I didn't want to encourage the guy and here we are, talking like we're best friends or something. "Hey, I'm sorry about last night, Jensen can be a bit *protective.*"

"No shit. He's like a fucking raging bull. So I've not got a chance then?"

"No, definitely not. Thanks, but no thanks and all that. I'm happy how my life is right now. Care free and uncomplicated." I laugh at him, and he gives me a warm smile in return. If only he knew how much bullshit was pouring out of me. I never used to lie, but now, it's like second nature to me.

"Fair enough. You can't blame a guy for trying. Fancy showing me around? I promise, just as friends?" I study him closely, to see if he has an ulterior motive, but he seems okay. I guess there isn't any harm in giving him a guided tour around a public place?

"Yeah, sure why the hell not? I've just got to nip to the library for something, and then I'll be free for a few hours."

"Awesome. I'll wait for you in my car. I'd rather not freeze my balls off."

"You not coming in? I thought that's why you were here?" Normally I'd be questioning his motives right about now, but I remember what it was like to be the new person in town. He's probably been stood outside here for hours, debating whether or not to take the plunge and sign up for something. If I didn't have Holly around when I moved out here, then I don't know what I would have done.

"Nah, maybe I can find something else to pass the time. Plus learning isn't really my thing."

"Well, I'll won't be long, and if you don't mind waiting, then knock yourself out."

Jed and I spend the afternoon walking around the local park and the more time that I spend with him, the more I find myself warming to him. He's told me that he's had to move out here suddenly to be with family after his mother's sudden death, and my heart goes out to him. I don't know what I would do if anything were to ever happen to my dad. That's the main reason I moved out here myself, to protect him, to make sure he remained unknown to the ones that I was running from. I don't tell Jed any of this though. My private life is solely private and no one else's business but my own.

"It's been really nice getting to know you, Anna." Jed says to me as I climb into the passenger side of his car. Maybe I'm being a bit reckless by getting into his car when I don't really know him, but he seems alright to me, and I've actually enjoyed spending some time with him today.

"Yeah, you too." I smile at back at him.

"Maybe I'm pushing my luck a little, but what about you and I do this again, sometime?" His thumbs tap against his steering wheel as he waits for my answer.

"Do you know what? That doesn't sound like such a bad idea." It finally feels that I'm making new friends around here, and that makes me happy. Hopefully, with each day that passes, everything else will eventually fall into place.

"What the fuck are you doing driving around with that guy?" I've literally just walked through the doors of Temptation and Jensen is storming towards me, his face twisted up in a heated rage; looking like he's about to go psycho at any fucking moment. He looks kind of hot, all worked up like this, but I know now isn't the time for fun and games.

"He dropped me off at work, what's the

big deal?"

"What's the big deal? I'll tell you what the big fucking deal is. You don't fucking know him. He could have done anything to you, and there's not a fucking thing that you could have done about it. I saw the way he was fucking eyeing you up and down last night."

"Jensen, you need to learn, that I don't need you to babysit me. I'm a big girl and I can sure as he'll look after myself." I push past him to put my things away, but he grips me tightly on my arm and draws me back.

"Yeah? What would you have done if he turned out to be some psycho? What would you have done then, huh? Shit, he still could be for all you know."

I don't know why he's getting so worked up about this. Taking in a deep breath, I look at him and say, "He's new in town, and he wanted someone to show him around, that's all. I remember what that was like, Jensen. Turning up at a town, that you know nothing about, and none of the fucking people in it. Not everyone's like you, you know."

"What the fucks that supposed to mean?"

"Well look at you. You turn up out of nowhere and you don't give a shit who likes you. You're happy being by yourself, and you get on with your day to day business regardless of what else is going on around you. Not everyone functions that way Jensen." I shout. I try to reign it in, but I'm really struggling here.

"Don't be getting in a car with someone

you don't know again, you hear me? If you need a ride anywhere, then you call me."

Now he's starting with his bullshit demands. I thought I made it pretty fucking clear that I won't put up with him bossing me around. "I've told you before, do not tell me what to do. You don't own me, and you sure as hell can't order me around."

"I've got my reasons, Anna. I'm not prepared to let anything happen to you, is that too fucking hard for you to understand?"

"I get it, jeez. Nothing is going to happen to me. I don't take meeting new people lightly Jensen, but it's fucking high time that I made some new friends around here." His hands work their way up my neck, until his hands are bunched in the back of my hair.

"Are you ever going to listen to me?" His tone is pleading and I have no response to his question. He shakes his head then pulls me closer to him and, all too suddenly I'm consumed by him once again. I know what he's doing and it's not going to work. He's trying to persuade me, or to help me forget about my new little friend. If I ever thought that I was paranoid, then Jensen's on a completely different level altogether.

"Well, it looks like we've got this place to ourselves for a little while." His temper has vanished and he's got a devilish glint in his eye, and all too soon, I decide to let our little disagreement drop, *for now.*

"Really?" I whisper against his lips.

"Mmm mmm, and I've missed you just a little bit too. I guess it's not good when our fun was cut short this morning, huh?"

Suddenly my mind is replaying unwanted images of Minnie storming into the kitchen this morning, with me in nothing but Jensen's t-shirt. "I don't think I'll be able to face her again, after that. It's too embarrassing." I admit to him.

"Sure you will." His breath is warm against my neck as he laughs. "You've got the same parts, haven't you?"

"Yeah, but what I mean is, if she'd arrived any later it could have been one hell of a different story." I shudder.

"That it definitely would have been, but it would have been a pretty fucking awesome one. One, that, she definitely wouldn't be forgetting in a long time. Now about this place and us..."

"Aren't we due to open soon?"

"Not anymore." I watch his fluid movements as he walks over to the doors and bolts them shut. "You seem to forget that I'm the boss, and I'm the one that makes the rules, Miss Jameson."

"Is that right?" I ask, smiling as I slowly step backwards to get away from him. I'd be lying if I said I didn't want him, but here? In the middle of the bar, I'm not so sure. He knows what I'm doing and he looks like he's having none of it.

"Don't walk away from me Anna. If you do, it'll only get worse." There's a hint of play in his tone, so I don't take him too seriously, but continue to walk backwards and crash into the bar behind me. As soon as my feet are stationary, I'm lifted up on to the bar in one swift movement. The power in those arms, sends shivers of pure bliss though my body and I don't think I ever want it to stop. His deep dark browns search mine before he leans in to kiss me. "You're my fucking obsession, Anna, and there's not a goddamn thing that I can do about it. I've tried my best to ignore how I feel about you, but it's fucking killing me" I feel myself murmur against him in reply. If only he knew I felt exactly the same. He leans over me and reaches behind the bar, searching for something, but I'm not sure what. When he leans back, the smile on his face is nothing but pure, danger and I couldn't be more excited at what he has planned for me.

"Now, I don't like it when people don't listen to me Anna. When I say something, I like to think that they respect me enough to listen to what I have to say.

"I'm not following you…" I say, he's making no sense whatsoever, but Jensen cuts me off mid-sentence.

"Do you like disobeying me, Anna?" his hand pins both of my wrists together behind me, while his other hand begins to circle my nipple, with something cold. The pleasure is absolute torture, but I know that if I cry out, he'll pull away and leave me like this, just so that I'll happily beg for more. I look down and see, that the item he pulled from behind the bar is a cube of ice, and I watch as it slowly melts from the heat of my skin, and he smiles his wicked smile as our eyes connect. "You're mine Anna. From this point here on out, you're fucking mine. This body, these tits, and this fucking mouth of yours, it's all mine and only mine."

My throat is dry and firmly closed, from the feelings that are rippling through my body. How does he expect me to talk to him, when I can't even think straight? Even if I could talk, right here in this moment, I wouldn't even know what to say.

ANNA

I know I'm walking around with a dopey arse grin on my face and I don't care. Joey keeps looking at me like I've lost my mind and he'd be right. My whole body feels lighter, and for the first time in a hell of a long time, I don't feel the pressures of worry weighing down my shoulders. Who knew that Joey could be right at something? It looks like finally letting my hair down and having some fun is working wonders for me.

"Have you been doing some of those shots again? You know, you don't mix well with them, Anna." Joey looks at me with worry in his eyes, and that makes me smile even brighter. I am happy with the people in my life right now and I wouldn't change them for anything.

"Ah, shut your mouth. Can't a girl smile every now and then?"

"Yeah, of course, but this is you that we're talking about Anna. You're normally out to rip people's balls off. So what's changed? Oh my god, you got laid, didn't you?"

"Come on Joe, that's none of your goddamn business, so quit it."

"Oh, you so did. So who was it? Was it that hottie from last night? You're secretly a kinky bitch aren't you? I fucking knew it, and I can't believe you haven't told me any of this." He sounds genuinely hurt that I haven't confided in him about my mystery guy, but in all honestly, I haven't gotten my own head around it all yet. I mean, what does he expect me to do? *"Hey Joe, you'll never guess what, but Jensen fucked me senseless last night..."* Somehow, I don't think that's appropriate for work talk, friend or not.

"You're getting way ahead of yourself sunshine."

"Speak of the devil. Looks like lover boy just can't stay away from you and that fine body of yours."

"Piss off." I look over towards where Joey's eyes have landed; and I see Jed coming straight towards us. If Jensen sees him here, he's going to flip his shit, but he can't stop me from talking to people, especially while I'm working. I know he's off doing some guy shit with Boyd, but I just hope for Jed's sake that he doesn't come back anytime soon.

"Hey you. Fancy seeing you here." He greets me as he walks up to the bar and his dimples stand out as he smiles at me. It's pretty contagious and I find myself smiling back. "I thought I'd drop by and have a drink before I disappear for the night. I didn't expect that you'd still be working."

"Neither did I, but shit happens. Well what can I get you?"

"Just a beer for me, and whatever the beautiful lady fancies." I raise my eyebrows at him and his hands shoot up in surrender. "What, I can't help it. My momma always taught me to tell the truth, so I speak the truth."

"I'm flattered, honestly, but I thought we said friends?"

"Yeah we did, but I still pay a compliment where a compliment is due. I don't mean anything by it, I promise." I can't stop myself from laughing at his comical expression. He actually seems like a decent, down to earth genuine guy. For reasons that I can't explain, I feel really comfortable around him. Normally I'm anxious as hell around new people, but he's quite soothing. I feel my face heat when Joey walks past and whistles in our direction.

"So where's your beefy bodyguard tonight?"

"I don't have a bodyguard, but he's around, I'm sure." If he isn't back soon, I'm sure he'll have someone reporting back to him while he's away. At the thought of Jensen, my face beams brightly. To onlookers, it probably looks like my smile is for Jed, but that couldn't be any further form the truth. Hopefully Jed will finish his drink and leave before Jensen spots him. The way his attitude was earlier, I don't think he's likely to hold back from him if he sees him in here talking to me.

"Why don't you come and have a quick drink with me? Surely you're due a break right?"

"I am, but I'm pretty busy here and I can't really leave the bar understaffed." It's not a complete lie, but it's not exactly the truth either. To be honest, I don't want people gossiping and getting the wrong idea, especially Joey.

"I'll keep the bar covered, girl. You go and enjoy yourself." Joey winks, while his eyes show what's really running through his mischievous mind.

"I'm good, honestly."

"Go on Anna, you're always behind here. Go and let your hair down for five minutes."

I've seated myself right next to the bar, so that I can jump up and help out at a moments notice. Sure, not many people will need serving in a five minute period while Joey's manning the bar, but I hate being away from my workload, especially if it's not work related.

"You're not from around these parts are you?"

"Um, no. Is it that obvious?" I ask, a little taken aback, while sipping on my diet coke.

"You're accents different is all. So where are you originally from and why did you end up here?"

"I don't know, I guess I just fancied a change." What a strange question to ask someone. There's not a chance in hell that I'm getting into this with him. Only Holly knows the full reason for me moving here and she soon disappeared out of my life.

"Really? You just upped and left everything you know because you fancied a change?" I know he doesn't believe me, but then again, he doesn't have too, but there is no way that I'll be telling him any different.

"Yeah." I don't like the way this conversation is heading, it's making me feel a little uncomfortable. "Do you usually ask so many personal questions when you first meet someone?"

"Oh man, sorry. I'm a douche. I guess I'm a bit too inquisitive. I'd never be able to just up and leave, that's all I'm saying. If my mum was still here, I'd still be at home doing my usual nine to five. Please don't be offended, I just get curious to know more about people."

"Well I didn't just up and leave. It's been my life long plan to move out here. I've been saving up for it, for as long as I can remember." I lie, but I need to get this dude off my back. Inquisitive or not, it's down, right rude to pry into someone's personal life whether you know them or not. "I'm gonna have to head back to work, it's getting pretty busy, but it's been good talking to you again, Jed."

"Yeah. You too Anna. Who knows, maybe

I'll see you around. It looks like this is becoming a regular thing, us two bumping into each other." His face lights up as I smile back at him. He might be nosey, but he seems like an all right guy, none the less and nobody's perfect.

"It sure does, doesn't it."

"Oh that guy's got is so bad for you. So, how was it, getting down and doing the dirty after so long?" I watch Joey, as once again he has his beer bottle in hand, while looking glazy eyed.

"Joey, I'm gonna say this once and only once, stay the fuck out of my business, and quit drinking all the goddamn beer while you're at it."

"You're so fucking touchy. Why don't you want people to know? It's not like he's ugly. He's like your own Prince Charming, and, girls go crazy for dimples right?"

"Know about what?" I hear Jensen before I see him and I want the ground to open up and swallow me, so that I don't have to face him. How much of that conversation has he just heard?

"Anna's got a new fuck buddy, and it's about time too." Joey chimes in.

"Is that so?" I look at Jensen and my face heats up under his gaze. His eyebrows are knitted together with confusion and I'm lost for words. All I can do is look back at him, hoping he'll understand that Joey has gotten the wrong end of the stick.

"Damn straight. What's his name? He's just been in to check on his beau. It's pretty sweet really, seeing as only the other day she was drier than the desert downstairs. But now that she's back on that pony, she's raring to go, ain't that right Anna?"

"You wanna watch your fucking mouth." Jensen snaps at Joey and I can tell he's beyond pissed. "Is this true? That guy from last night, has he been back in here?"

"Yeah, He stopped by for a quick drink or something, so what? It's a bar Jensen, you know, where people come to have a drink..."

"And stare at what isn't fucking theirs." He's shouting now and I can feel the weight of a dozen eyes penetrating me as I stand here having a show-down with the boss.

"I don't belong to anyone, Jensen. What the fuck gives you the right to tell me what I can and can't do? Who I can and can't see? Nothing, nothing gives you that goddamn fucking right." Now I'm shouting and I don't care who hears me. Jensen steps that little bit closer to me and I can see his chest moving rapidly and the veins in his neck threatening to burst from the anger that he's holding in.

"If I fuck you, then I sure as hell don't share you. Plain and fucking simple." He turns his back on me and shoves Joey out of the way before disappearing into the office and I've never felt so angry and embarrassed in all my life.

"Happy hour has started." I shout out to the crowd. "And I'm about to start it off." I line up a couple of shots on the bar and pour the amber liquid into them. "Once they're gone, they're gone, so what are you waiting for?" I'm the first to pick up a glass and down it, but deciding that one isn't going to be enough, I then take another, and then another before grabbing my bag from the side and walking out of Temptation for what I feel is going to be the very last time.

JENSEN

I watched Anna leave the bar through the CCTV and I couldn't care less. I don't share chicks. If they're screwing me, then they shouldn't even be thinking about other fucking guys. I've never tolerated it before, so why the fuck would I tolerate it now? The one thing that pisses me off even more, is the fact that she didn't even try to deny it. Now that's a fucking guilty conscience if ever I saw one. I pray to god that I don't have to see that guys face again, because the way I'm feeling right now, I'll end up ripping his fucking throat out. I warned him to back off yesterday and I fucking told Anna that I didn't appreciate her wandering around with a guy that she doesn't even know. I know that makes me a hypocrite, but I'm not some random guy. I'm Anna's boss, and she's living in my house, so that gives me a bit more leeway than a complete stranger. The guy looks like a cock too. He's not worth my time and energy, so why am I sitting here dwelling on it?

"Has Anna been back here?" I shout over to Joey as I lock up the office behind me.

"Nah, I haven't seen her since she stormed out earlier. Hey, listen pal, I'm sorry if I caused any problems before. I didn't mean anything by it. It's just that Anna has been acting more care-free recently and I kind of went to far."

"Don't worry about it, just make sure you tell me the next time that guy comes in here. You okay to close up? I'm gonna see if I can find Anna." I hate the thought of her wandering around this town on her own. I know she's managed perfectly fine before I came along, but I also know that she's scared as hell from whatever it is that she's been running from. I still can't remember the guy's name that Mitchell was going on about, but if he's a screw-loose, then I sure as hell don't want her walking the streets on her own.

The lights are off when I pull up in the drive. Maybe she's gone to bed in a foul mood. If you're going to lie to someone then you need to be prepared to face the music. Luckily for her, I'm too fucking worked up to demand answers from her, so for now I'll let her sleep. Hopefully I'll feel better once I've had some shut eye too. My rooms not your average bachelors pad by any stretch. All that's in here is my bed and a couple of boxes containing my life. I move around a lot, so I don't see any point in holding onto shit that's only going to weigh you down along the way. Plus, it's how I like my life these days, plain and uncomplicated. Well at least it was until I met Anna. That chick seriously does something crazy to my head. I've never known anyone like her. She's so independent, yet I know she's fighting some battle on the inside. I just don't know what it is yet. But I'll make sure that I find out what it is, and when I do, there's no way that she'll be able to hide away from me anymore.

I'm woken to the sound of a doorbell. I don't know what time I finally crashed out, but it can't have been that long ago. All I want to do is go back to sleep, but whoever it is doesn't seem to be calming down anytime soon and they're fucking persistent. I glance at my watch and see that it's nine-thirty in the morning. This better be fucking important for their sake.

I open the door and see Minnie, dressed up to the nines itching to come inside. "What the fuck are you doing here Min?" I ask, unsure if I can cope with her drama this early in the morning, without a trace of caffeine in my system.

"I'm going to see Mitchell. I thought I'd

stop by and see if you wanted to come along and see him yourself?" Stepping back to let her past, I notice that she's really pulled out all the stops for today. Her dress is so short, that she's practically wearing nothing and she's decided to team it up with fucking fishnet tights. I hate to say it, but she looks like she's just come back from working the streets all night.

"You know they don't let you fuck there, don't you?" I ask her, while lazily walking into the kitchen.

"Of course I do. What do you take me for? I haven't seen him in so long J. Is it so bad that I want to give him something to look forward to, for when he comes home?"

I always knew Minnie was crazy, but I'll never understand her. If I was stuck where Mitchell is, there's no way I'd be thinking of what was to come when I arrived home, instead I'd be too busy wondering if that's how she dresses all the goddamn time when I'm not there. Now that, that shit would get me in more fucking trouble which would prevent me from getting home to her sooner. Luckily for Minnie, Mitchell's never been the jealous type, and anyone who knows Minnie, knows she's loyal to my brother to the core.

"You want a drink? There's no way I'm leaving this house until I've woken up properly, especially seeing as though I'm gonna be sat in a car with you for over an hour. You know, you could have called me last night to give me the heads up or something."

"Hey, get your finger out of your arse, I only found out this morning. There's been a mail strike or something and thankfully it arrived today, otherwise who knows how long I would have had to wait for another one."

"I know you miss him Min, we all do. But, you know he'll be home soon and then you'll get him all to yourself for a little while."

"He can't go back J. You know he can't go back right?" Her face is panic-stricken as the thought goes through her frantic mind. I've never known anyone to care about my brother as much as Minnie does, and it's good to see. No matter what they've been through, and they've been through a lot; they always stick together.

"I know. He isn't gonna be going back. He can stay here until he's fixed somewhere, and then when it's time for me to move on he can have this place. Don't you worry, I've got it all worked out up here." I say while tapping on the side of my head.

"Good, I'm glad someone has. I didn't think you'd be moving for some time, especially now that you've got *little Miss Pretty* to come home too?"

"Who, Anna? Nah, I don't think that's enough to keep me in one place. You know me, times change and shit moves on. As soon as this boat's sailed, I'll be gone." As I say it, I know that it's utter bullshit. I know that Anna has fast become my anchor, and wherever she is, that's where I'll be. But how the fuck do I admit that out loud, that's my problem. I look up and see Anna stood in the doorway. Shit, I didn't even know she was there. I can tell by the pained look on her beautiful face that she's just heard every word that I have just I said, and I wish I could take the words back in a heartbeat. I try to say something to her, but nothing comes out. I just stand here looking like the complete, heartless bastard that I really am, and there is nothing that I can do about it.

"Hey Anna, you want a coffee? Jensen's about to make a pot in a minute." Minnie says, as if she's sensed my sudden discomfort.

"No I'm good. It's time that this ship sailed anyway." *Fuck, fuck, fuck. Say something Jensen, just say something."* I'm stood frozen on the spot as she looks me up and down like I'm some piece of shit that she's just stepped in, and then she turns those mighty fine legs right around and storms away from me for the second time, in less than twelve fucking hours.

"Looks like someone's in the dog house." Minnie whistles.

"No fucking shit." I want to go after her and explain that, what I said, came out wrong so, so wrong and to tell her that, that's how I used to be. Fuck, I was a lot of things before Anna came in to my life, and most of them I ain't proud of.

"Leave her be, she'll calm down soon enough, you'll see?"

"Yeah? You don't know what she's like. She'll go back to hating me and wanting nothing more than to painfully remove my balls every time she sees me. When she's got one on her, it ain't fucking pretty, Min."

"J, quit over thinking it and get ready. She's a woman. Sure she'll be pissed at you for a while, she'll probably bring it up in all of the future arguments between you both, but she'll forgive you eventually. You've been blessed with the Blake charm; you boys can get out of any shit, anytime if you really put your mind to it."

"You better be fucking right, otherwise I'm holding you responsible for this. If you hadn't come around, then I would never have had to explain myself, and Anna would still be here, right where she belongs."

"I get it, you've never done this before, and that's perfectly understandable, but now you know how it feels to care for a real woman. It takes a lot of work too, so don't think that once you guys have worked this out, everything will be all pretty flowers, because you and I both know that isn't what life's about. You've got to work hard for what you want, and what you believe in J. Why do you think Mitchell and I have lasted this long?"

After whipping my sorry arse into shape, we pull up into the parking lot, just over an hour later. "You sure that you're ready for this?" I ask Minnie, before I cut the engine.

"No, but it's not like I haven't done this before, is it? I just wish that he'd stop getting caught up in other peoples shit you know?"

"I know. He's not always innocent either Min. He's my brother and I agree with you completely, but when he's home, he really needs to get his life back on track. If he's certain that he's done with this lifestyle, then all we can do is be there to guide and support him along the way."

"He knows that. I guess it's a hard habit to break. I know that's why he sent you away when things got bad last time. Most of the stuff that he has done, is because he's been too busy looking out for other people instead of himself. This time I'm gonna make dam sure that it doesn't happen again. Jeez, J. Mitchell and I should have made you an uncle by now."

"Really, so when he's home, I'm gonna get some baby making sounds coming through my wall every goddamn day? You know I'll do everything I can to keep him out of trouble." I say, before giving her hand a comforting squeeze. Minnie's been in my life for as long as I can remember. Deep down, I know the crap that she says is for my own good, but coming from a woman; sometimes it's a little too hard to handle.

Mitchell is sat at the same table where he was sat last, when I came to see him. His hazel eyes light up at the sight of Minnie and his face looks younger and care-free. Now, that right there, is the Mitchell that I love. My older brother, who would catch me when I fell, or bandage me up if he was too busy getting it on with Minnie when he should have been looking after me. My brother, who I ran home to after school with my achievements and high grades and who I would also cry to when the older kids thought it would be fun to pick on me. As soon as Mitchell got involved, they didn't think it was much fun anymore.

"Hey baby. I've missed you." He says to Minnie, and she beams back at him.

"Right back at you beau. It's so good to finally see you. I can't wait for you to come home."

"Baby, when I'm out of this place, make no fucking plans, because we've got a fucking lot of catching up to do."

"Hey guys, I know this is sweet and all, but do you mind?"

"J, I'm in the middle of something here. You don't like it, go sit outside until visiting time's over."

"Are you being for real?" He can't be fucking serious. "I've not come all this way to watch you two practically fuck each other. Tell me what you told Boyd and Minnie and then I'll leave you both to it." I'm beginning to wish that I'd never come with her now, whatever has happened obviously isn't bothering him, so why should I let it bother me?

"I'm sorting it, don't worry. It's not as bad as I initially thought, plus it looks like the jerk has fell off the radar anyway." He waves it off with a flick of his hand. If Mitchell's happy that it's all under wraps then that's good enough for me.

"So what's the plan?" I ask him, unsure if he's heard any news, yet.

"I'll be home by the end of the week, little

brother." His face is a picture of pure happiness, and Minnie has tears streaming down her face.

"So, I heard him right? He's actually gonna be home by the end of this week?" She say's for the third time since we left the prison.
"That's what he said"
"I'm so fucking excited that I get my baby back. I could squeeze you so tight right now."
"Do that and I'll fucking disown you." Minnie jabs me in the arm, playfully. She knows that I'd never do that to her, and if I'm honest it's good to see her finally looking so happy, after all this time.
"I cannot wait to get than man home; and back in my sheets where he belongs."
"I think you'll find that they're my sheets, and you guys better do your own fucking laundry." The last thing I want to be rifling through is their bodily fluids, dry or not.

ANNA

I find myself sat in the nearest coffee house, alone with my mind on overdrive. I knew that if I let Jensen get close to me, that he'd drop me as soon as he could. I've not felt so humiliated like this in a long time, and now I feel like once again, history is starting to repeat itself. I knew we were getting on too well for things to continue to run so smoothly. Yes, we had a little run in last night, but that could have easily been resolved. Fucking Joey, and his mouth. One of these days he might just learn to keep it shut. Maybe if I'd actually done something with Jed, I'd kind of understand Jensen's reaction, especially after the way I acted towards him with Darcie and Minnie, but I didn't do anything other than be polite to someone that needed a friend in an unfamiliar place.. There's no need for me to explain myself to him, and if I'm being totally honest, if Jensen thinks he can try and stop me from talking to, or meeting the people that I want to, then he's completely barking up the wrong fucking tree. At least I finally know where I stand with him, just another notch after all.

"You mind if I join you? You look like you could use the company." Jed sits down opposite me and smiles sweetly in my direction, displaying those cute dimples. I wish I could smile like that and feel as happy as he looks right now.

"Sure. I supposed I should be getting worried that you're turning into some kind of stalker now or something?"

"If only I was, I guess that would make my life sound a bit more exciting than it actually is right now. The truth is, I had some errands to run, so, I thought I'd do them all in one go. Who knew being efficient could actually be fun?"

"Tell me you're taking the piss? I can't think of anything worse." I laugh, suddenly feeling a sense of ease bouncing from him.

"There we go; at least one good thing came out of today."

"What's that?" I say, unsure where he's going with this.

"I managed to make you smile."

"Thanks. I needed it. So what are you really doing around here?" It does feel weird that wherever I go, he seems to be popping up out of nowhere, all the time.

"I was telling the truth when I said I had a few errands to run, and then I saw you in here and I thought you looked a little down. I thought you could do with cheering up."

"I've just got a lot going on right now that's all. I'll be fine as soon as my caffeine fix kicks in, I didn't get chance to grab one this morning."

"Well, how about I do one better than that? Let me buy you lunch? It's the least I can do to say thanks for welcoming me to the area. If it wasn't for you, I'd probably be sat at home, drinking and smoking myself into an oblivion to escape the boredom."

"I think you just got yourself a deal, Mister."

The more time I spend with Jed, the more I like him. He seems like a down to earth kind of guy. Someone you can talk to, without the fear of being judged. Also, we've got a few things in common too, such and our music tastes and films. It's also nice to know that I have someone to talk to, if I need to get out or if I just want to vent. However, I'm not ready to test that theory on him just yet. I think my explosive past would be enough to scare anyone away and at the moment, I could do with all the friends that I can get.

"Thanks for lunch, it was... Nice."

"Anytime, like I said; I appreciate the friendship."

"What's really happening with you Anna?"

I'm never going to escape people wanting to know about my past. I must have a look that says, *"Oh shit, you better watch this one. She comes complete with a shit load of baggage."* Every single person that I meet, sooner or later wants to know more about me, and as much as I like the people that I have come across while I've been here, that baggage isn't being unloaded. Ever.

"I've already told you mine. It was my dream to move here." I laugh a little at his scrunched up face and I know he isn't buying it, but that's all I'm giving him.

"Everyone carries around secrets with them Anna. It's nothing to be ashamed of, you know. Look at me, mine's a long story. Bottom line is, I lost someone close to me and decided that I couldn't stay there any longer. Too many memories you know"

" I know, and I'm sorry."

"Don't be, shit happens. The best I can do is to try and rebuild my life and where better to start than somewhere new? And the best part is that I get to do that with you, because I know that's exactly what you're doing, for reasons that you're not quite ready to share just yet, and I'm completely fine with that." I look out onto the sidewalk and wonder if Jed and I have more in common than we actually realise, other than music and films. Sometimes all you can do is run away to escape your past, otherwise, all it will do is drag you down until there is nothing left of the person that you once were before.

        "It's been nice." I say again, and I mean it.
"Next time I'll shout lunch, but I've gotta head
back. I've got heaps to do on my assignment
and I don't want to fall behind. I don't want my
tutor to kick me off this course. I need it too
much."

        "I get it; it's getting pretty dark out there
now, how about I give you a lift back? At least I
can rest easy knowing that you got home safe,
and that big beefy protector of yours won't come
looking for my balls."

        "You don't need to do that, but thanks for
the offer though." I can't help the anxious feeling
that's growing within me. I don't know why,
because I know he's not going to try anything.
I'm pretty sure he would have done that by now,
especially since I have been in a car with him
before. Maybe it's because, secretly, I know it
will only result in another slanging match with
Jensen if he sees me getting out of Jed's car.
Then my mind flickers back to this morning,
listening to the hurtful comments that he made,
and I want him to hurt, I want him to feel pissed
off, and realise that my doesn't start and end
with him.

        "I know I don't need to, but that way I'll be
able to rest easy tonight, okay? Please let me do
this, even if it's only to say thank you."

        "Okay, but I don't want you going out of
your way."

        "Jeez, has anyone ever told you how
much of a nightmare you can be? Come on, let's
get you home." The car journey isn't as awkward

as I thought it would be. Instead, both Jed and I sing along to the radio as if we've known each other for a lot longer than we have. He's actually pretty funny and downright entertaining. My eyes are streaming most of the way home from laughter, and my chest feels light, something that I haven't felt unless I have been around Jensen.

"Tell me to mind my own business, but what's really happening with you and your boss, Jensen, isn't it?"

"Mind your own business." I smile at him, which causes his dimples to deepen. "There's nothing much to tell. Oh I don't know. It's way more complicated than it needs to be."

"You're telling me. I thought he was gonna bust my knee caps when I first met you. So you're not together?"

"No, we're definitely not together. I guess he just likes to take care and protect his own, that's all."

"Bullshit. A guy doesn't act like that just to look out for his staff. That other chick who was working with you was getting eye-fucked all over the place and he didn't even bat an eyelid. I think maybe he's got a little soft spot for you."

"I can promise you now that he most definitely hasn't. Plus, it wouldn't matter much anyway, now that he'll be leaving soon." I stop once I've realised what I've just said. Saying those words aloud make it seem much more real and my chest aches at the thought of me never waking up early again just to bump into him as he leaves the bathroom in nothing but a tiny towel. To know that our heated arguments will be gone forever, hurts me more than I thought possible. Why, oh, why did I let myself succumb to him? I knew I was letting myself in for a massive fall.

"He's moving? What's going to happen to the bar?" Jed seems quite interested in what I have to say, as he turns the music down a notch.

"He'll probably sell it, I guess. Why, are you thinking of buying it?"

"Maybe. Hey, now that's not a bad idea. I wonder if you could speak to him for me? He might be more likely to show up if you do the talking instead of me."

"Yeah, I suppose I could ask him. I've got your number in my bag somewhere, so I'll call you and let you know what he says." Jed has a valid point. I think if he called Jensen to discuss selling the bar, he either wouldn't show, or he'd turn up and do him some damage to prove a point. Jed waits until I am out of the car and making my way up the drive, before he restarts the engine. As I turn to wave at him, he's busy on his phone. Bloody hell, he doesn't waste any time if he's calling someone about the bar. Oh well, I guess that I'd rather have Jed running Temptation, than a complete stranger.

"How do?" The voice that I have been needing; yet dreading to hear at the same time greets me as I walk into the kitchen. I didn't expect Jensen to be sat at home. I thought he'd be too busy at Temptation, or planning his new life as soon as his boat is ready to sail, but here he is, brooding in his favourite spot at the table. "Hey." Is all I manage to get out, I'd love nothing more than to walk over to him and feel his hard solid frame against mine, but he banished all rights of me doing that this morning. Instead, I toss my bag down and walk over to the refrigerator.

"Anna, about this morning..."

"Don't bother explaining, Jensen. It's fine. You always said you weren't gonna be here for long, and it was pretty stupid of me to think otherwise. You do what you need to do; just don't let me get in the way."

"That's not what I meant. Jeez, will you just sit down and listen for once?" I weigh him up for a minute, undecided and torn and still upset from his words earlier. "Please?"

"I'll give you five minutes Jensen, but that's all."

I sit down on top of the table to keep my distance, but he throws out his arms and drags me towards him, so that his arms are firmly placed around my hips. I like the look of him sat in this position, between my legs. He looks vulnerable and nothing about the hard nut exterior that he normally wears, shows.

"I'm sorry. I was so pissed off when Minnie turned up out of the blue this morning, and she just wouldn't stop with the questions. I'd been awake for five minutes max and I know that doesn't excuse what I said. Shit, when she brought your name up, my answer was automatic. An answer, that I would have said before I met you. Plus, the last person that I want to witness me go soft over some chick is Minnie." He never breaks eye contact with me as he says this, and his hands run firmly around my hips in circular motions, as if he's checking that I'm still here.

"You sounded pretty sure to me, and convincing." I'm all over the place. I have no idea what he's trying to tell me. He likes me, but not enough to stay, or for me, he's going to stay.

"I'm a convincing guy when I need to be Anna. I've learnt that the hard way, there's no doubt about it. What I'm trying to say is, for the first time, in for as long as I can remember, you make me feel like I have a home. You make me feel wanted, and I sure as hell don't want this feeling to stop. Yet, at the same time, you drive me fucking insane like no one else, and I need to know what you're doing and when. I need to know what's going on in that pretty little head of yours, because not knowing what you're thinking is killing me."

"So what you're saying is, you're a little bit of a possessive control freak; that just wants to be loved?" Smiling at him, his face grows darker and I immediately wish that I'd dropped the sarcasm.

"Do you know what? This is fucking bullshit. I didn't sign up for this shit Anna. I'm trying to tell you how I feel and you're just sat here laughing at me?"

"I'm not laughing at you Jensen, I was trying to lighten the mood a little. You're the one who's getting all up in arms about everything." He pushes himself back, away from me and stands in the middle of the floor, his hands gripping his hair in frustration. All I can do is sit here and wait for him to say something. Eventually, he turns to face me, anger blazing like an inferno in his deep brown eyes.

"I'm not good at this Anna. I'll only end up tearing you apart. One way or another, you'll be left broken, and it will all be my fault. I'm a selfish son of a bitch, and although I should stay away from you, I just can't do it. You're in my mind, every goddamn minute of every goddamn day. You possess my whole being and I'm utterly, obsessed by you."

"Jensen, I didn't sign up for this either. God, I've tried, but I can't walk away from you. I really wish I could, for my own sanity, and I'm scared, scared to let you in. Scared of how I will feel if I lose you, and scared that a few months, maybe years down the line; you'll suddenly look at me and think, what the fuck have I done. *Even more so of what you will find along the way.*" I say the last sentence in my mind, but it still eats away at me as if I've said it out loud.

"These lips, they're mine. This body, it's only mine, and here," he holds my hand across his chest, "is something no one else has ever had before, and it's all yours for the taking." I reach up on my toes and place my lips against his, missing the connection of us together.

Pleasure instantly powers through my body at his touch and I never want this feeling to end. I snake my hands around his neck, so that I can pull him in closer to me, desperately wanting to keep him this way for as long as possible.

"I've missed you today."

"You have?" I ask, smiling against his lips. "It's only been about eight hours."

"An hour is like pure torture for me." He pulls his head back to look at me, searching my face deeply, for what though, I have no idea. "What did you get up to?"

"I went for a walk. You know, to try and clear my head. When I was at the coffee house, I bumped into Jed..." I instantly feel his body tense at his name, but if he's going to be sticking around, he's going to need to get used to the idea of me having friends around here, whether they're male or female.

"I don't like him Anna." No shit. I really didn't get that from how he acted last time.

"Why, because there's just something about him or is because he's male and you don't want him around me?"

"I see the way he looks at you Anna. No one should be able to look at you like that apart from me, you hear?"

"Excuse me?" Now he's not making sense.

"He looks at you like he wants to devour you. That's my job. He looks at you like he's fucking you with his eyes. That again is my job, and I get the pleasure of doing the real thing after, no one else. Do you need me to go on?"

"Nope." I smile at his worried face. "I think you've made it loud and clear. But just so you know, I'll still be seeing him; he's a friend, nothing else. So deal with it."

"I'm not fucking happy about this, Anna. The minute he tries anything, I'll hunt him down and take a sizzling fucking poker and ram it in his japs-eye."

"Well you don't have to be happy about, you just have to deal with it, and violence never solves anything, does it?" I lean up once again and plant a kiss onto his cheek and hope that all is forgiven. "Anyway, I'm gonna hit the shower."

"Want me to join you? I'm sure it would be more enjoyable with me in there, I'll make sure I give you a thorough scrub down."

"I think you need to set off for work, otherwise you're going to be late."

"Wouldn't want the boss to find out about that, would we?"

"I don't know, you might want to watch yourself. I've heard he's very *firm* yet fair and he's pretty hot too. He might make you self-conscious ."

"Oh yeah? Shame I don't dig guys, otherwise I'd be right in there. So are you telling me this from experience?"

"Get out of here." I shout, trying to usher him out of the door, while laughing at the shocked expression on his face. Tonight turned out much better than I ever imagined it too, and I'm going to bed one happy lady.

ANNA

    I'm surprised to find the kitchen empty. Normally Jensen's already down here, brooding away over whatever goes on in that head of his. Maybe he's gone out for a run, or he could still be in bed. After all it's still pretty early and I didn't hear him come home last night, so it must have been late. My phone chimes to life on the table beside me, and I look down and get a sudden pang of fear as I see an unsaved number flash across my screen.

    "You need to stop worrying Anna. When will you realise that you're safe here? If anything was going to happen, it would have happened before now." I quickly slide over the answer button and place it to my ear, but the line is quiet

on the other end. There's not a chance in hell that I'm speaking first.

"Hello, Anna? You there?" My body relaxes at the sound of Holly's voice and I allow myself to breathe again.

"Hey. How are you?" I ask, thankful to hear from her.

"Someone's mood has improved. Does that mean that I'm finally forgiven?"

"No, but being mad at you isn't going to change anything is it?"

"I knew you'd see sense, all I had to do was give you some time to calm your arse down."

"Don't push it Holly. So what's new? Where are you now? Are you still having the trip of a lifetime?"

"Well, that's why I called actually. It pains me to say it, but maybe I didn't think this through properly." You've got to be fucking kidding me, I think to myself. Suddenly she doesn't like it, now that she has left everything behind.

"Why, what's happened? Is everything all right?"

"Chill out, you worry too much. Everything's fine. It's just money doesn't last does it. It looks like we'll be coming back much sooner than we thought." I knew there had to be a reason to her calling me, out of the blue. Holly was never one to just call for a quick chat.

"What are you gonna do? You don't have a home anymore Hol, or a job for that matter." I remind her, and I can hear her shocked intake of breath down the line.

"I'm not stupid Anna. That's where I'm hoping you could help me out. I wanted to know if you could talk to Jensen for me. You know, see how he feels about giving me the house back?"

"Let me get this straight. You want me to ask Jensen if you can have your house back, after you and that Hernandez have spent the money that he paid you for it? You're some crazy chick Holly. There's no way he's gonna go for that, you know that right?"

"How do you know if you don't ask him?" She pleads down the phone to me, and I can't help but feel a tiny bit sorry for her.

"Because any sane person isn't going to give up a house for free, Holly. I must have grown up blind to miss that people do that."

"But I made a mistake and I want to come home, Anna. Is that so bad?"

"Well, you're just gonna have to deal with this one Hol. I'll speak to him, but I can hear his laugh already. It's completely up to you if you want the colourful version of the conversation that'll take place? Maybe this will be a lesson to you."

"I'm sure you could persuade him Anna." I know instantly what she's implying and there is no way that I'm having this conversation with her, especially over a goddamn phone.

"Right, Holly, listen. I'm gonna have to shoot, I've got some stuff that needs doing, but be careful out there and I'll call you on this number later, once I've spoken to Jensen, okay?"

"You got it. I'll speak to you later. Thanks Anna, I owe you big time."

I place the phone back down and can't believe Holly's cheek. She's the one up upped and left, whilst in the throes of passion, selling her home and the bar; only to decide now, that she made the wrong decision. To me, that's not something you can't come back from. No one in their right mind is going to hand back a business and a property without getting the money back that they paid for it in the first place.

"Hey. Is there any coffee going spare?" Minnie asks as she steps into the kitchen. She seems to be here all the time, why I'm not sure, but everywhere I turn, there she is.

"Sure is." I reply back to her, as politely as I can.

"Where's Jensen?" She asks, as she looks about the place, searching for him.

"I don't know. He's either in bed or gone out for a run or something."

"I didn't hear him come home last night, that's all." Minnie looks panic stricken, and although she's trying to hide it from me, I can tell she's worried about something.

"Is everything all right, you look worried?"

"Yeah, of course. It's just not like him not to return home, that's all." My mind instantly goes to the worst possible explanation. Maybe he ended up running into the arms of Darcie if the temptation got too much for him, or worse some chick in the bar came onto him and he couldn't resist her charms. I feel sick at the thought, and can no longer stomach my coffee.

"I'm sure he'll come waltzing back in when he's good and ready."

"Yeah, I hope so." I say, while hoping that my thoughts aren't true. What if Jed went to Temptation and they got into a fight? No, that can't be right, as surely Darcie or Joey would have called to let me know.

The morning goes by slowly and I find myself pottering around the house, waiting anxiously for Jensen to return, but he doesn't show. Minnie looks out of her mind with worry and asks me heaps of questions around his whereabouts and if I'm familiar with any other places that he visits.

"The only place that I know he goes to is here and Temptation. What about his friend Boyd? Maybe he could have crashed there?"

"Maybe, I doubt it though, he would have been home by now. Jensen isn't the best sleeper around and you can bet your arse that no matter where he's been, he'll always be back home by six-thirty in the morning."

"You know quite a lot about him." I say, more to myself, than Minnie.

"Sure I do, I've grown up with him and I've been dating his brother for the past thirteen years. There isn't anyone who knows Jensen better than himself, other than me and his brother."

Our conversation is quickly brought to a stop as the phone rings beside us on the table. Neither one of us reaches out to answer it, and it's only when I realise that it's left to me to answer it, that I find the strength to move.

"Hello."

"Anna, hey it's Darcie. I know I'm the last person that you want to speak to right now, and believe me the feeling is mutual, but it's about Jensen, and you're the only person that I could think to call…"

"What about him?" I snap down the line at her. Hearing his name coming out of her mouth makes me feel sick. I knew he wouldn't be able to stay away from her, it's not like she's shy when it comes to flaunting herself ether. Any hot-blooded male could be swayed by a half-naked slut waltzing around you noon and night. Shit.

"I was wondering when you saw him last. He never turned up for his shift last night, and Jensen doesn't do AWOL. He *always* arranges cover first and informs someone, that's just how he is."

I look over at Minnie, as an icy dread fills the pit of my stomach. What if something bad has happened to him? How would we even know where to look for him? "Well thanks for calling to let us know. I'll call you if I hear anything." Placing the phone back on the hook, I don't even know where to begin.

"Who was on the phone, Anna? Is it Jensen, is he okay?"

"That was Darcie, she said Jensen never turned up at Temptation last night. She sounded really worried too."

"So she should be. That's not your typical Jensen behaviour. He's never a no show unless he tells someone, that way people don't need to worry about him if he's not around."

"Why would people be worried about him?" I ask, feeling a sudden fear of danger for all of us. What have I gone and gotten myself into now?

"Oh, Anna. Jensen and his brother haven't been innocent, hardworking people all the time you know. Surely you knew that right?" Secretly, somewhere deep inside me, yes I did know, but I chose not to tar everyone with the same brush as me and my past. All I can do is pray that he walks through that front door in one piece.

JENSEN

Fuck, my head hurts. I can feel it thumping with every shallow breath that I take. I try to open my eyes, but it hurts too much. What the fuck happened? My head feels like it's about to split in two and I have no idea where I am, fuck I'm even more clueless as to why I'm here.

I try to move, to sit up, something, so that I can get a better feel of where I am, but I come across my first hurdle. You've got to be fucking kidding me. I struggle to get up as my wrists are bound, and so are my feet. This had got to be some kind of fucking prank. It's so dark in here, and I can't see shit. It's cold, so fucking cold that I can just about make out my breath in the air every time I breath. I try to think back, to think of the last thing that I can remember but everything's coming back blank from when I opened up Temptation. I don't know if there was a fight, I don't even know if anyone knows where I am. It's all one big fucking mystery.

"Hello? Hey, is anyone there?" I shout, getting fucking agitated with each passing minute that's ticking by. If this is Boyd's idea of a joke, I'm gonna take his fucking balls off and watch as he chokes on them. "I know someone's there. I can hear you fucking breathing. Come out so I can see your face, instead of hiding out in the dark like a pussy."

Everything remains quiet for some time and I only hear the deep shallow breath of my captor to keep me company. All of a sudden I'm on high alert as I hear the unmistakeable sound of a revolver clicking into place, followed by footsteps somewhere in the distance. I start to panic on the inside, when I realise that the longer I sit her, it's becoming more apparent that my kidnap wasn't a prank after all.

"Wakey, wakey, baby Blake." The voice without a face says to me. I've never heard that voice before, but I sure as hell don't like it.

"Who are you?" I demand, sounding much more confident than I feel.

"It doesn't matter who I am, Jensen. What matters is that you are here. You and your brother are impossible to track down. Always on the move, or locked up in prison. But now I have you right where I fucking want you, and it's time that you paid for what your brother has done to me and what he has taken away from me."

"You're making no fucking sense here. I haven't got a fucking clue who you are, or what you want?" As he comes closer to me, the air is filled with a pungent smell, stale alcohol mixed with smoke and damp, and I have to fight back the nausea that overcomes me.

"I want what's mine, and I will get it, one way or the other, and that fucking shit dick of a brother of yours will get what's coming to him."

"How the fuck do I fit into the equation? I don't even know what you're banging on about." This guy's on some other fucking level. I've been taken against my will, because he has some kind of vendetta with me and Mitchell and I don't even know what the fuck he's going on about.

"Let me spell it out for you. You're brother fucked my life up not so long ago, and I ain't the type of person to let that go. I've been waiting for the perfect opportunity to make him pay, and here you are, his little baby brother, who he'd do anything for. He gets released from prison this week doesn't he?"

Who is this guy and how the fuck does he know what's been happening with Mitchell? He sparks a match to light his cigarette and I catch a glimpse of his face. "Who are you?" I ask again, but he doesn't say anything, he just laughs.

"Did your brother ever mention his dear old friend, *Dominic*?"

You've got to be fucking joking me. As soon as he says his name, I remember, that this is the guy that Mitchell was trying to warn me about, as well as Boyd and Minnie. They must have known he was on the hunt for when Mitchell was released. But he said it was all under control. Fuck, fuck, fuck. Now I'm stuck here, trapped with this psycho, unable to escape. I just fucking pray that someone notices I'm missing, and manages to track this son of a bitch down before I end up six feet fucking under. I feel a sharp blow to my head, and my last thought is Anna's face, her perfect fucking face, looking at me through hooded eyes, before the darkness sweeps over me.

ACKNOWLEDGEMENTS:

It's that time again, where I would like to thank you all for supporting me, patiently waiting on ARC's to finally hit your kindles, following numerous formatting Issues, and so on.

I would like to start by thanking my sister, for feeding me and supplying me with endless amounts of coffee every day. Sure, you moan about it afterwards, but I know you enjoy it really.

My ladies, again, you have been amazing. It still amazes me that you take time out of your day to post my teasers, buy-links, anything that I post you are willing to share and that means the world to me.

Charisse, what can I say? This is the first time that we haven't shared a release day and I don't think I like it all that much. Next time we need to make sure we go back to how it was. I need my partner in crime back, and fast!

Lastly, I would like to say a massive thank you to you; my readers, for buying this book and my previous stories. I love hearing your feedback and I hope you have enjoyed reading the beginning of Jensen and Anna's story.

ABOUT THE AUTHOR:

Welcome to the crazy and hectic life that is me... A fun, loving mum of one special little boy, girlfriend (I'm sure it should be wife by now!!) and an overall crazy, happy go lucky girl from England.

I have always had a passion for reading and writing. Wherever I am, my book reader is never far behind along with a mug of coffee.

I found myself wanting to write from a young age, I have quite a few hidden stories on my computer somewhere; maybe I will have to dig them out and play around with them at some point.

Follow S.M Phillips here:

www.facebook.com/sphillipsauthor

www.twitter.com/s_m_phillips_

Printed in Great Britain
by Amazon.co.uk, Ltd.,
Marston Gate.